At Reception

At Reception

A Short Stay in Sally's World

Galahad Porter

Matador
9 Priory Business Park,
Wistow Road, Kibworth Beauchamp,
Leicestershire. LE8 0RX
Tel: 0116 279 2299
Email: books@troubador.co.uk
Web: www.troubador.co.uk/matador
Twitter: @matadorbooks

ISBN 978 1788032 711

British Library Cataloguing in Publication Data.
A catalogue record for this book is available from the British Library.

Printed by CPI Ltd, Croyden, London
Typeset in 11pt Adobe Garamond Pro by Troubador Publishing Ltd, Leicester, UK

Matador is an imprint of Troubador Publishing Ltd

To Laena and all guest service agents,
my thoughts are with you.

AUTHOR'S NOTE

At Reception is a tale of self-discovery and transformation. It's the story of Sally, a hotel receptionist. Set at the desk in a hotel lobby, the novel follows Sally over three days at work.

When Sally arrives at work at 7am she sees a young girl, Lily, standing alone in the middle of the lobby floor. This sets off a flood of memories and thoughts that will change her single life forever.

As a receptionist Sally has to be nice to everyone and accept orders from management, whatever her thoughts and needs. In seeking to deal with her personal issues, Sally finds herself in a lonely world of her own making. Suffering psychological stress, unsupported and untreated, she chooses to live alone, with only stuffed toy 'pets' for company. Unable to change her situation, she is locked in a cycle that's impossible to escape and cripples her life.

Unable to express herself at work, she uses her hair ribbon to communicate externally what she feels emotionally and sexually. With no close friends, Sally discusses her issues with the flowers in the vase on her desk. On the wall opposite her desk is a large lobby mirror, making her self-conscious all day long. Her interactions with guests are punctuated with conversations with both the flowers and herself in the mirror.

Every day is a series of short interactions with guests and staff. The guests provide the basis of a series of short stories which intertwine through the book over the three days. The guests range from young to old and represent many different lifestyles, from very single to happily married. Characters include an old-fashioned gangster, a cookbook writer, a fading sports star, a cruise ship charmer and the 'resident' prostitute.

Sensitised by Lily, Sally's interactions with the guests increasingly challenge her long-held opinions and self-image.

One of the joys of writing is the ability to describe what a character is thinking and feels. In *At Reception* I have taken this to an extreme, using the first person, where everything is from the perspective of the main character. The reader gets to see the world of hotel reception exclusively from Sally's perspective, and experience what she really thinks in parallel with the conversations she has with guests at the desk.

At the end of the book I have reproduced my blog posts from my website, chronicling the tortuous process of writing *At Reception*. The evolution of the writer is as important as the novel itself!

A special thanks is owed to Laena Blauw for introducing me to the world of hotel reception.

Galahad Porter, January 2017.

www.galahadporter.com
Twitter: @galahadporter
Facebook: www.facebook.com/GalahadPorter or @GalahadPorter
Email: info@galahadporter.com

EVERY WORKING MORNING AT 6.55AM

It's a red-and-black checked ribbon day. Like every working day, at five minutes to 7am, Sally looks in the hotel staffroom mirror. She draws her hair up into a ponytail, then carefully folds and ties the ribbon into a perfect bow. Glancing over her make-up and earrings, she touches up her lipstick, and finally checks there's nothing left from breakfast on her teeth. She holds her red-painted nails out against the cover of her mobile phone, then a glance again in the mirror, and with a little pout the nails are checked with the lipstick, all three a perfect match. Adjustments are made to her black jacket and white shirt – they've got to look just right, the shirt buttons in a perfect line. Twisting her black knee-length skirt, she twirls a little to make sure the zip is in line with the middle of her back. A further turn and she scans her tights for runs and tugs and, finally, looks down at her plain black, flat, comfy shoes for scuff-marks. Happy everything is as perfect as possible, she opens the staffroom door and walks down the short corridor towards the lobby door.

MONDAY

CHAPTER 1

GOOD MORNING!

At exactly 7am, five days a week, Sally opens a concealed door into the hotel's marble-and-mirror lobby. Feeling nervous, like a gladiator entering the ring at the Colosseum, unsure of what she will face, she checks herself one more time in the large wall mirror across the lobby from her desk.

'Good morning, mirror!'

Yes, it's definitely a red-and-black checked ribbon day! Red nail polish, black panties and black tights. Not a spotty or stripy day. Just a normal old day for me to get through. Done it many times, so no worries today.

'Good morning, flowers!'

Good, Matt's still at the reception desk after his night shift. But why is there a young girl standing alone in the middle of the lobby at 7am?

'Hi, Matt, what's that girl doing in the lobby at this time?'

'Oh, really? I'm not sure, I never noticed, I was busy cashing up.'

'She's coming over here.'

I wonder what she wants, she doesn't look upset. Where are her parents?

'Good morning, how can I help you?'

'I saw you talking to the flowers. Why do you talk to them? They don't have ears so they cannot hear you!'

What do I say? Why do I talk to the flowers? It's been a long time since I confided in a human. I always found them unreliable and two-faced. I would tell school friends secrets, and the next thing, everyone was laughing at me. I found over time that human relationships were usually painful. Flowers never cause me anguish, except when others hurt them. The mirror never lies to me. It never says, 'You look great, go out in that dress' and then I get ridiculed by everyone when I'm out with so-called friends. The flowers and mirror are all I need.

'What's your name?'

'Lily.'

Ah, what a sweet name.

'Lily, I am Sally. The flowers can hear. Just because you don't have ears doesn't mean you cannot hear! When I talk to them they feel the vibration, and hear that way. Obviously they cannot talk back, but that's OK, I think I know what they would say.'

'How?'

'Because they are my friends. You always know what your friends are thinking, don't you?'

'My mummy says she can read my mind!'

'I am sure she can. Some people hug trees. I am sure it makes the trees feel better, and helps the people too, I am told.'

'Mummy says I mustn't go near strange people who want to hug.'

6

Oh my. There goes innocence. But I know all about scary hugging in childhood. I still suffer the consequences.

'That's quite right.'

'There's Mummy, she's finished in the toilet, so we can go to breakfast now.'

From an early age, all the way through my younger teenage years, my parents sent me to religious summer holiday camps, mainly to get me out of their hair. I hated it. Nobody understood my ideas, they didn't even want to listen. When I first went they listened patiently and explained their views, but later, no. They told me I was wrong. I couldn't work out how they could say that, what they said did not make any sense to me. The moral principles sounded good on the surface, but the explanations behind them seemed just plain crazy to my mind. Everyone is free to have their own religion, their own beliefs. I wonder if all religious groups are like the one I had to suffer. Probably not – maybe I just hadn't found the right one. I felt like I was ignored in favour of those who agreed with what they were told. Then there was the physical contact. All that hugging after a service made me uncomfortable. Old men touching me, squeezing up to my breasts. I hated my parents for making me go through that. I wonder, why are the little girl and her mother up so early? Why was her mother in the loo, having just left the room? Presumably she went for a pee there, just before coming down. I am sure she would have made sure her daughter did!

'Thanks for hanging around, Matt, how was last night?'

I know he wasn't waiting for me, he normally rushes off. Guess he was just late cashing up.

'Boring, no hooker game I'm afraid! She came in, according to Katie, just after your shift but left after about forty-five minutes. So there'll be no betting on which guest she stayed overnight with! Sunday night was a bit quiet, no groups yesterday.'

'Did she do her usual, getting the guest to distract reception as she sneaks out of the lift?'

'It's pointless her doing that, we all know her game. But it's funny watching the guest come up to the desk with obviously made-up excuses with which to try and distract us. Katie didn't say which guest it was, so I can't tell you who to try to embarrass by asking if they had a good time rather than a nice stay! Anyway, gotta rush, there are a few things in the night logbook to look at. The man in 1703 died, but it's all been dealt with. But make sure you watch out for the guy in 1308, the whinger room!'

Matt has always 'gotta rush' when there is shit lurking around but yet to hit the fan. I wonder what it is this time.

'Is Frank about? He's supposed to be working with me as duty manager this week.'

Don't tell me I'll have to deal with everything alone, yet again.

'No, you know management! Oh, there goes Mr 1308 off to breakfast. Bet he'll be here in a few minutes with a complaint! Have you seen the new notice? Bye!'

Yes, I wonder what is that in the frame? Why's it cluttering up the desk? I stand in the middle, flowers to my left, mints for guests to the right. That's all that is allowed on the top of the desk. Nothing else confusing things, messing things up, spoiling the picture.

The Hotel Management will not tolerate any abusive language or behaviour by customers towards its employees. Signed, *The Management.*

What idiot put that there? Has the boss, Mr Temple, seen this? Maybe he put it there? Surely not. He knows how I like things, he always says he understands me. Mind you, since his management course he's gone weird, and seems to have forgotten all our names. 'Its employees' – who does he think he is? I'm not owned by him, nor by the hotel! And what's with 'customers'?

'They are guests, in fact my guests, not bloody customers. This isn't a supermarket!'

Oops, I didn't see someone was standing there – the damned notice is already causing me problems.

'Good morning, how can I help you?'

'What were you shouting about?'

Shouting? Shit, I thought I was muttering!

'It's a notice the management have put on the desk.'

It's actually a really stupid notice for guests, saying not to abuse us or else!

'What does "will not tolerate" actually mean?'

'I haven't a clue!'

It's supposed to intimidate you guests into having a nice attitude. I don't want it on my desk. And the frame is awful, it doesn't go with anything! Why are so-called 'important' signs put in old-fashioned gold frames? It doesn't match the flower vase, or the mint bowl, or my nails or the bow holding up my hair, not even the lobby decor or our black uniforms!

'Well, I agree: people should be nice to you!'

'Thank you.'

But my job is my job. The guest is always right, so they always have the right attitude. My job is to be as tolerant as possible, as understanding as possible, and keep everyone happy and feeling special. No matter how much of a shit they are. I smile, or look concerned, or use another appropriate expression, and give an answer to please them.

'Can I help you with anything else?'

'No, thank you.'

That it? Why did you come to the desk in the first place? I bet you forgot! It's a stupid notice and I don't want it on my desk. It'll just encourage sarcastic comments, and won't change people's behaviour. Someone may even want to hit me with it! It's going under the table!

'There we are, flowers, let me move you back to where you go. The notice is under the table now, safely out of your way. That's better, isn't it? Do you know, flowers, in the northern hemisphere it's snowing and the holiday season? Here summer is approaching and brings with it my birthday.'

Celebrations are not a part of my life. Living alone, with no family and friends, I only share special times with my stuffed toy pets and those poor animals at the rescue centre. At work we occasionally exchange gifts, but it's not personal, it's work. As much as my colleagues feel like family when I am here, I know they are not. They are never at my home. As I am paid a minimum wage, my rent and bills use up all my money. The glamour of the hotel is not the reality of life for the workers. My simple existence is all I can afford. Not having to buy gifts is one less stress in my life. I am happy to keep it that way.

Well, here we go again, another week at work, another week like all the rest in the year. Definitely a red-and-black checked ribbon day today! Nothing in my life has changed in the last week, month, even years. Every week like all the others. I don't mind that, I know where I stand. No doubt this week will bring a new set of events, characters, chat-up lines and challenges to exhaust me. Having to be nice to people all day, which I take seriously as it is my job, is mentally tiring. The constant barrage of having to say one thing but really thinking another is tough. Flowers, you know me, when I get tired I am tempted to let rip, but I always seem to hold on and just make it to the end of the day without upsetting anyone! I'll be OK, I will make it through, I've had the weekend to recharge my batteries. No doubt on Monday next week we will be having the same conversation as we always do! So, let's see what's in the night book.

The guy who died in 1703 had a heart attack. Let's see… yes, he was fifty-nine. Poor bugger, too young. I bet he spent his whole life looking forward to retirement and never got there. Imagine working all those years and the golden days are taken from you. Sucks. I wonder if he was with the hooker? No, with his wife. Poor thing. She'll be shattered by this. I guess she'll be too old to easily get a new man. The rest of her life, maybe fifty years, alone. I'm happy alone, but she'll not be used to it. It will be a big adjustment for her. I hope she has some family for support – not like my family, a real family. Hope Matt checked them out… good boy, but he charged them for the room anyway! Bastard. Too chicken to make a decision himself, and no doubt the night manager

Craig wasn't around at the time. I imagine he would have been 'supervising' by chatting with the ambulance guys whilst having a cigarette. I'd better check with Maria that housekeeping have cleaned up properly!

Now let's see, what else? A no-show – well, better call them.

'Hello, it's Sally at reception at the hotel. You have prepaid for a room for two people for three nights but have not checked in yet. Are you still coming?'

'Prepaid? I didn't know that!'

'It's your credit card.'

'What? Bitch!'

'I'm sorry, sir?'

Did he just call me a bitch?

'No, not you. My ex-girlfriend! She said she had booked a surprise, but I won't be coming.'

'Will she still be coming?'

'She better not! We split up two days ago!'

'Oh, I am sorry.'

'Not half as much as I am! Using my card! Bitch! Bet she planned it that way!'

'I'm afraid the room is a non-refundable rate.'

'What? I can't get a refund?'

'I might be able to change your reservation to another date, should you wish?'

'You joking?'

'Just trying to be helpful.'

Oh, he hung up. Who's the bitch now?!

'You see, flowers? That's what I get for being considerate.'

But I would never change my job. You know I love the

idea of travel, although I have never been abroad. Working at reception in a hotel feels like travelling, with all the tourists, businessmen and people on trips coming and going to the airport, and of course, the cruise ship passengers. Their stories make me feel part of it all. Of course I could never travel abroad. I don't have the self-confidence or money to do that. I am happy with my routine, my job, and get out of it what I can cope with. My holidays are at home, with little visits to nearby places I know, especially the animal sanctuary. I empathise with the poor things. Nobody gave them a notice in a gold frame about not being abused. They have all suffered, you can see it in their eyes. Mind you, if I had a relationship I could travel, as I would not be going alone. The problem is, that whilst there is no shortage of suitors, it's difficult finding someone I feel comfortable with. I've lived alone for a long time now.

'Flowers, will this week's batch of chat-ups be any different? Probably not!'

OK, what else do we have in the night log? Who's this guy in 1308? Mr Wilson. What? How many complaints could someone possibly make? If he's after a discount he's gone way over the top. Surely his stay can't possibly be that bad! He's even moved rooms twice, claiming the bathroom mixer taps didn't work in the first one, and the air conditioning didn't work well enough in the second! In this room he says it's not clean enough, room service didn't collect his tray, which was smelling the room out, the bar guy Peter ignored him when he was waiting to be served, the restaurant didn't have what he wanted and wouldn't make it for him. No wonder they moved him to our whinger room. Room 1308 is a special room. Historically it's had the most complaints, and Maria in housekeeping thinks it is haunted. As whingers will complain anyway there is no point in trying to please them with a nice room. So now I put Whinger of the Day candidates into it deliberately, and the complaints become a self-fulfilling prophecy.

'As usual, flowers, I'm the one who has to try to make whingers leave the hotel happy when they check out in the morning!'

I can't wait. I am loyal to the hotel, it is my family, my life. I hate it when people criticise the hotel and staff. I feel very defensive when they do. Obviously, like family, I am allowed to criticise the hotel and staff as much as I want, although I keep staff criticism largely to myself – I have to work with them!

*

I'm so happy they have changed the telephone system so it flashes rather than rings. No more *ring-ring* all day, echoing around the lobby and in my head. Trying to help a guest with the phone shouting at you is hard.

'Good morning, Sally at reception speaking, how can I help you?'

'This is Mr Jones, room 1304.'

Oh, he sounds serious.

'Good morning, Mr Jones, how can I help you?'

'There is something under my bed!'

'What does it look like?'

'A dead mouse, but it's a bit bloody.'

'Oh dear, I do apologise for that. I'll get someone to come and remove it for you. I'll send housekeeping up right away.'

A blood-soaked mouse corpse! How did that get there?

'Maria, it's Sally. The man in room 1304 says he has something under the bed he wants removing. Said it's a bloody-looking thing with a tail, probably a mouse.'

'He looked under the bed?'

'Yes.'

'Why was he on the floor looking under the bed?'

'Not a clue.'

'Nobody ever looks under the bed! Everyone knows it's dangerous, they even made a scary film about that!'

'He looked under the bed, can you send someone up to take it away?'

'A mouse, you say? We don't get mice at that level. Sounds like a used tampon!'

Very funny, Maria!

'Yuck!'

Bet he thinks it's a tampon and is too shy to say it. I wonder how that got there. Dread to think what was happening in the room!

*

Ooh, someone is getting a large box delivered to them!

'Hi, I have a delivery of flowers for Sally at reception.'

'That's me. Thank you.'

A dozen red roses in a box. You have to say, 'a dozen' as florists never say twelve! But no way, in a box – it's like a coffin for the flowers. They need light! Flowers should be in water with a clear supporting wrap held together with a bow! So who's it from? A machine named Douglas by the look of it! The fake handwritten card printed by a computer. *Thank you, Sally, for making my stay so nice. Lots of love, Douglas xxx.* Douglas… oh, him – yes, he stayed three nights last week. But I hardly chatted to him, just work stuff. It's my job to be nice to all guests, even ones I don't like. So why do people assume I am interested in them? I might be a real shit outside work, not their type at all. My smile at work means nothing more than politeness. Nothing to deserve three kisses. He wore a brown suit, brown shoes and cream shirts with a patterned brown tie. He was nice enough, but looked insipid, he could have been carved from a log! A bit more white in his hair and he would have looked like a latte coffee, an equally insipid thing! Brown and beige mean conservative, and an excess of them means boring. I would have to change him, and maybe that's what he needs, a partner to do that. I don't want all that work, I can do without that stress on top of everything else in my life.

'Flowers, a dozen roses shows his lack of imagination!'

I don't like red roses or chocolates as a gift, they have been debased by Valentine's Day. Why red roses? Everyone does that automatically at Valentine's, so it means nothing really, like sending a box of chocolates. What's the point? There is no real thought in the gift. Why not send a different type of flower, personally selected, in a colour with meaning? That would show someone had spent time with real thought and caring. Roses and chocolates won't get you anywhere with me, especially without a personal handwritten note! If you think you can get me by spending more time on a website typing in your credit card details than selecting the gift, forget it! A mixed bunch from the supermarket or petrol station doesn't work either. They look pretty but are meaningless, as the types of flowers and colours all contradict each other. You can have red and blue, hot and cold, which makes the combination tepid! A person sending flowers should go into a real florist and carefully select which flowers, with special meaning, should be in the bunch. Mind you, people need help, and you have to have a good florist, not the useless one the hotel uses! The coffin of roses can go under my desk for now until I decide what to do with them.

*

Aha, it's the guest from earlier who didn't want anything!

'Hello again, how can I help you?'

'Isn't it a bit early to have this music playing in the lobby?'

'It's on all day and night!'

'Nevertheless, I do like it! What's the CD?'

You don't have to listen to it several times a day for months on end!

'Oh, it's a compilation created by the manager, he loves it!'

'He has great taste, you must tell him!'

'I will!'

Won't. Is that what you wanted to ask when you came to the desk earlier? Are you just bored and have nothing better to do than listen to lobby music? It echoes around the lobby so it's not as if you can hear it that clearly, you need to be in the bar for that. The lobby noise is very irritating. The chitter-chatter of people, the tip-tapping of heels, the shrieks of children, the rolling of wheelie cases – they all get on my nerves.

*

Well, well, well. Creepy Alex the concierge is heading my way. Hmm, he's sauntering over here, not walking deliberately with a purpose. That means he is still not sure how to put the question that's burning within him. I bet he wants to know if the roses were a gift, and who sent them. He chats to all the delivery guys when they arrive, so he will know they were for me. Worse, he will want to know if they were a gift from a guest and then try lay claim to them, supposedly 'on behalf of all the workers in the hotel'. Alex never shares his tips or freebies, unless in return for something!

'Alex, what brings you to my side of the lobby?'

'Hi, Sally. You free for a drink later?'

Keep a straight face, don't laugh! This is not why he is here! He invites me out for dates all the time, but he just does not understand me. Maybe he is trying to be nice, but I doubt it. He could be jealous of the rose sender, mmm. Mind you, men do get jealous over things. He could be the possessive type, one of the jerks who think if they can't have you, nobody will. Spoilsports who'll try to ruin anything nice.

'I'm sorry, Alex, but my cat and I have an Italian session tonight.'

'That's a shame. I saw you received a big box!'

No, it's not chocolates. If it was he would want to force me to share them around. Come on, Sally, put on a big smile now.

'Yes, someone who really cares about me sent me roses!'

In a coffin.

'Roses? But it's not Valentine's.'

Bingo! That's what I mean! Some people have no imagination.

'You can send them at any time of the year! Not just Valentine's.'

'So who's the lucky guy then?'

None of your business.

'That's private.'

'You sure they are not from a client?'

Now he's getting offensive, and it's a guest, not a client, you jerk.

'No, now let me get on with my work!'

I hope I don't have lying eyes! Alex gets all the tips and freebies, the theatre tickets, discount vouchers, free meals. I only get compliments and guest comment cards! Reception is the hub of the hotel, not the concierge, although Alex thinks he is, and all reception do is 'process people'. I'm the one that usually ends up processing guest complaints about him, and have to come up with excuses on his behalf!

*

There go Lily and her mum after breakfast. What would life be like as a single mother? I guess it has the advantage of

19

not having to take into consideration another adult in the relationship. I wouldn't have to compromise with someone else, the child would be brought up in my world as I like it. Well, at least until they became old enough to want their own way on how things should be. On the other hand, there are the extra pressures of dealing with the needs of a child alone, especially before it can go to nursery school, having to look after it full-time. I could not afford to give up work, so guess single motherhood is not an option for me.

*

Nicole from the reservations department is on her way to get coffee. You can tell it's her, she is so pasty white. Because reservations talk all day on the phone they are locked away in their little room. It gets no sunlight, as that would make it hard for them to see their computer screens. No problem in my big, airy lobby, the design makes it light without too much direct sunlight. Her colleague Jack is all muscles and bronzed, so he must go to a gym and have sunbed treatments. They go for coffees a lot, so I guess they feel the need to get out of their room – either that or the job is really boring.

'Nicole!'

'Sally, hi! What's up?'

'I received a box of roses from an admirer. Now, I don't like red roses, so thought you might want them?'

Isn't Sally a nice girl?! I can also rub home the point that, even without a partner, I do have a fan club.

'Really? An admirer, that's a surprise.'

Don't go there.

'Just don't let Alex know about it! You must take them home today, they are in a box so make sure you hide it!'

'Great, thanks, Sally!'

*

At last, a wide-awake guest with a purposeful look. Some are still bleary-eyed at this time of day.

'Good morning, how can I help you?'

'Jones, room 1304.'

'Good morning, Mr Jones. I trust housekeeping cleared whatever was under your bed?'

'Yes, thank you. It was quite a fright!'

'What did it turn out to be?'

I just have to know.

'It seems it was a pair of red earplugs on a cable, the type people use with their mobile phones!'

'I wonder how they got there? Probably some kid hid them deliberately to get back at someone!' Kids do that kind of thing. 'Apart from that, I hope you had a nice stay and we hope to see you again soon!'

What was he was doing on the floor? Looking at him, it's hard to imagine he'd be having sex on the floor! Maybe he got drunk and woke up there? Got drunk and fell out of bed? Also, he called early this morning, not last night. If he called shortly after going to the room I'd have to assume he was some fussy guest checking for dust everywhere as soon as they are in the room, copying what they have seen in some reality TV programme! Hmmm, I wonder what he was up to?

'Flowers, it's a windy day outside today!'

Even you are getting a gust of breeze now and then! What do you think, mirror? It's not a good day for long hair without a bow! Every time the lobby doors open everything gets blown about, and leaves and rubbish from outside are blown across the floor. You too, mirror, you seem to be wobbling a bit – better get maintenance to come check you out!

'Hello, this is Sally at reception. The lobby mirror is wobbling when the doors open, can you come take a look at it? We don't want it falling down, do we now?!'

No, mirror, there was nobody on the line, that was the answering machine. You know maintenance never answer their phones! They claim they are busy with their hands. But I reckon they have coffee and doughnuts in them, not tools!

CHAPTER 2

HOW WAS YOUR STAY?

Why's the hotel general manager, the big boss, staring at me from across the lobby? Here he comes. Deep breath.

'Good morning, Mr Temple!'

'Where is the notice?'

And good morning to you too, you miserable sod.

'I put it under the desk.'

'Why?'

'It's not needed.'

'It's a great idea. Shows I care for our GSAs. HR agree.'

Well, if human resources say it does, it must be true. Not! You stopped caring about us after that management course. I bet that's where you got the idea from – you don't have the imagination to dream it up! Since that training programme we no longer have names. I am a GSA, not Sally at reception. A guest service agent sounds like a petrol pump attendant. I feel like I'm working in some management textbook, not a hotel with real people!

'I don't need it. I get on well with guests.'

'Put it back out. It will protect you from abuse, you may be pleased to have it one day!'

23

A lot of good that will do to protect me! Do I have to use it as a weapon against abusive guests?

'Do I have to? It doesn't go with anything on the desk.'

'I expect it back out by the time I get back to my office. I can check it's there on my security camera monitors.'

The shit. This is really going to piss me off. You ugly, stupid sign. Where do I put you? Let's see… so, mirror, what looks best? By the bowl of mints, I guess, I'm not having it spoil you, my flowers.

'I am so sorry, flowers, that the evil notice is back out.'

I know it spoils the desk. I'll have to put it at the end of the desk behind the mints so you and vase are not affected! You can still be seen by all as you are meant to be!

*

Here comes Peter the barman with my coffee!

'Hi, Sally, your espresso macchiato as always. I'll pop it by the computer for you, I know you don't like anything on top of the desk!'

'Thank you, Peter!'

I love the way he says, 'espresso macchiato', he sounds so Italian. He says it deliberately every time he brings it to my desk, he knows I like to hear him say it. It's such an exotic name, I am sure it makes the coffee taste nicer. I love it! When he was a student he spent a summer touring Europe, and in Italy he learned how to say it properly. He told me it means 'spotted' or 'stained', but I don't care. It sounds so good.

'I see you got the notice back out on the desk. I saw you hide it, naughty girl!'

24

'Yes, Mr Temple insisted I put it back.'

'I've got one too. There is little enough room on the bar as it is.'

'Especially as Ms Wilks seems to spend a lot of time perched next to it!'

'Oh, that woman. She is such a pest. I mean, she is not unattractive, but I am just not into women the age of my mother! Every time I look at her I think of my mum. I even said something like, "My mum has a similar handbag" and she ignored it. I can't do anything to put her off!'

'She must want you for something. Looks like she is heading towards the bar now!'

'Better go.'

I keep the coffee out of sight of the guests, once you have had a sip the cup looks a mess, with lipstick and coffee drips. The only problem with coffee is it stains your teeth. There is nothing worse than seeing someone with yellow teeth, especially on TV, which seems to make it look worse, as if the make-up department have touched them up too! Mind you, they look more natural than the brilliant white ones – they look so fake! I had a guest with brilliant white teeth once, and could not stop staring at them! Also, it's not nice having coffee breath when talking to my guests. As always, espresso macchiato time is followed by a quick mouthwash and lipstick reapplication.

*

There's a nice, steady flow of check-outs today. I hate it when there's nothing happening at the desk, time really drags.

But worse is a sudden rush, everyone in a hurry. As the line builds I can feel the stress. People muttering, sometimes sighing, and somewhere from the back a neck cranes out of the line. It's not my fault the system has issues, or when a guest cannot find their credit card in their bag. But not this morning. Maria will be pleased, she can get on with cleaning the rooms.

'Good morning, how can I help you?'

'I'd like to check out, here's the minibar list.'

'Apple, cinnamon roll, cheese sandwich and fizzy orange?'

'Yes, they weren't on the list so I added them.'

'But we don't stock these in the minibar.'

'You must, they were there!'

'Oh dear, it looks like someone left their packed lunch behind when they checked out!'

'Will it have been safe to eat?'

'Do you feel ill?'

I bet you will now I said that.

'Not at the moment.'

You'll say you were later, and you'll tell management all about it, hoping for a refund!

'Housekeeping restock the minibars in the afternoon, so I am sure everything would have been from that day. They remove anything that shouldn't be there! Let me call them.'

'Oh, I haven't time for that, the bill, please.'

'Well, we won't be charging you, the previous guests have already paid for it!'

'I should hope not!'

Glad they've gone. Better call Maria in housekeeping.

'Maria, it's Sally. Room 1606 left a packed lunch in the minibar and the new guests ate it!'

'What, they ate it?'

'Yes, they ate it!'

'Why did they eat it?'

'They just did.'

'Everybody knows not to eat things that shouldn't be in the minibar!'

'They thought it was part of it.'

'But it's not on the list!'

'I know.'

'They OK?'

'At the moment, but I am sure they will claim to be ill later!'

I hate people like that. I can't blame them if they see the chance to have something for nothing. But lying is downright wrong.

*

Here come a stereotypical family: husband and wife with two small kids! Why don't I have a husband and a little boy and girl? Mind you, they look miserable, so maybe I'm better off without! I wonder what's up with them.

'Good morning, how can I help you?'

'I know it's early, but my husband and I have been driving all night, and we really need our room!'

I wonder if hubby chickened or was pushed out of the conflict situation. Why do some women think they are better able to persuade a woman than a man? Maybe he told her that it's her fault for setting off too early, so she can sort the hotel out. All I know is he is silent, probably the safest thing to be under the circumstances.

'Check-in is from 2pm, but let me see which room you are in.'

'Please, we really don't mind which room. We really need to shower and rest!'

The kids look worn out. I bet the parents have been arguing all the way here. Why do parents always argue when they go on holiday? Is it the stress, the change of routine, or just having to spend all day, every day together? I feel sorry for the kids – all the anticipation of the holiday, then the excitement of leaving, and bang, the parents ruin it all. I know, I've been there myself.

'OK, I think I can juggle a few rooms around, it might take me a minute or two.'

'Oh, thanks, we are so grateful.'

I believe you really are. Nice killer stare at hubby there, I feel a 'told you so' coming on when they get out of earshot! No sex for you tonight, mister. Oh, there won't be anyway, they'll be sharing with the kids. That will up the tension between them even more! The young girl is hugging a stuffed toy lion. She looks like she needs cheering up.

'I see you have a lion, what's his name?'

'Richard.'

What? Who the hell calls a lion Richard?

'That's an interesting name, how did you choose it?'

'It's after Richard the Lionheart. I saw him on a film.'

'Oh, that's a very clever name.'

28

A lion called Dick. Did nobody dare tell her?

'I have a selection of stuffed toy pets. I have a cat – in the films they have cats in Italy. But I also have more exotic animals. I have a panda, they come from China. I have a tiger, they come from India. When I cook a meal with food from their country I let them sit with me on the sofa and watch TV programmes about their homeland.'

'Mummy, can I do that?'

'It depends what's on TV, it'll probably be past your bedtime.'

Send the kids to bed. Get them out of your hair as soon as possible of an evening! You didn't even tell her the meaning of the name Dick. I bet they giggle about her at school when she talks about Richard the lion. Some shitty boy will make a joke about 'dick' and think he is so clever. How many times did I end up being the butt of jokes like that? Too many to recall.

'Last night it was Africa! The giraffe enjoyed the safari. I could sense him straining his neck to get to the higher leaves on the trees in a wonderful documentary on TV.'

'What type of food do they eat in Africa?'

'It varies, it's a big continent with many different cultures. I am not sure what they eat where the giraffes live. I had a salad, leaves and all that! If the lion had been with me I would have had a steak. It's best just to have one animal at a time, I don't want them chasing each other!'

'That's silly. They are stuffed animals, they cannot chase each other!'

OK, clever so-and-so.

'They may not be able to run. But in their minds they do!'

'Mummy, do stuffed animals have minds?'

'Honey, I don't think they do.'

Don't stare are me like that! Let the child wonder, don't crush her imagination. Don't spoil a magical moment for her with cold, hard reality. Some parents have no idea how to bring up a child – no wonder they all play computer games, any imagination they had has been squeezed out of them.

'What other animals do you have?'

'Well, I also have a moose, they come from Canada. I have no idea what Canadians eat or watch on TV – probably cooking shows and soap operas like everyone else. Mind you, they know a bit about drinking in bars, I think!'

'We don't talk to the children about things like that.'

Talk to them? Yes, but do you really ever talk *with* them?

'Now, just let me see what I can find in the cupboard. I'm not supposed to do this… yes, here we are. It's not in your room rate, but here, let me give you children a kid's pack each, there's a colouring book, plain paper and crayons!'

'Oh, thank you so much! Children, what do you say to the nice lady?'

'Thank you!'

A grateful smile from Daddy there. I know what you are thinking. The kids can occupy themselves for a bit and take the workload off you.

Well, mirror, they looked like a nice family. Now I'm standing here all alone! Why don't I have all that: a husband and kids? What's wrong with me? Why am I not playing happy families? But do I really want a family?

'As I told you, flowers, I had a tough childhood.'

30

I never related to my brother or parents. That's why I moved to this coast to be away from them all. Maybe I am not the family type. I never get to see them as I cannot afford to travel there, and they never come here. I think my parents really only wanted a boy. Having me meant they had to have another go, and as they had a boy that time it was fine. He is only one year younger than me and they never had another child after him. When I was young I did not realise this and never resented it, we were just two kids doing kids' stuff. He seemed to get his own way more than me, but he was more boisterous. I was quite reserved, so put it down to that. It was only later that I realised some things seemed really unfair. He had birthday parties with all his friends, and I didn't. My parents said I was not good with other kids, so it was better not to. I didn't get it. He got much better birthday gifts than I did. My gifts were boring by comparison. I was told, 'He's a boy, and boys get stuff like that. You're a girl, play with your dolls.' Whenever we went out it was always to places he wanted to go. Whenever I said I wanted to go somewhere or do something he would always ask to do something different, and get his way. Eventually I started to rebel and my parents would separate us during the summer holidays. I was sent away to religious camps, supposedly 'for my own good'. By the time I became a teenager I felt sidelined, and really felt the difference in their behaviour towards us. As soon as I could I left home and got a job cleaning in a hotel. Whilst there I was given a chance to help out on reception, and met people who travelled. I loved it. They had a sister hotel with a full-time job vacancy on the other side of the country. I got it, and that's where I am now. I struggle, but I am in my space, my zone, my world.

*

'Hello. Excuse me.'

Oh, a guest.

'Good morning, how can I help you?'

'You were looking in the lobby mirror.'

Shit, how long was she standing there whilst I was thinking? I can't say I am worried it might fall down.

'I can't help it, it's directly opposite me.'

'That's nice, very useful in your job, I imagine.'

What?

'Not as much as you think. Imagine standing staring at yourself all day. All the things you notice that start to bug you, little flaws grow to huge proportions.'

'It's quite a way across the lobby, you must be in soft focus.'

'Thank goodness!'

If I could see every wrinkle… but under these bright lobby lights I can make out enough! I am self-conscious all the time. I keep noticing things about myself, and by the end of the day I have a long list of things that require further investigation in close-up. Is that good?

*

'Flowers, it's an hour now and no reply from maintenance!'

In life I find other people are always the biggest cause of stress. Not just in relationships, but at work, in the shops, in the street. In fact, everywhere. I particularly hate it when someone promises they will do something and they don't. I plan everything around knowing who will do what and when. I am dependent on other people to fix things around here. If people don't do their job it's an enormous stress. What can I do? Shout hysterically at them? I am sure that's not in management's manual as a motivational technique, at least not in this country.

'Hello, it's Sally at reception. I need the mirror looking at!'

Groan – still no reply.

*

It's a good thing I can see through the lobby's big glass entrance doors. My view goes past Alex the concierge's little podium to where the guests get dropped off and picked up. I get a warning if a person or a group is arriving, and know when someone has cleared off! But best of all, I can see the regulars arriving like clockwork. It must be ten o'clock already! Officer Hackness from the police station around the block is chatting to Alex. He always arrives at 10am exactly and chats to him whilst waiting for me to be free of guests. Then he'll come over and talk to me. He uses the excuse that he is looking for any suspicious behaviour, but I know he fancies me. Mind you, in this hotel everyone is suspicious! Even Officer Hackness. He likes to be called Officer. Nobody knows his first name. After a chat, he goes for a coffee at the bar and wanders out with a respectful nod and mini-salute to me on passing. He looks smart in his uniform, but I think he likes it too much, he really enjoys having a uniform. It makes him feel special, I guess. I hated school uniform, but it was the smartest clothes I had as a child. I feel sorry for poor kids having to go to schools where you can wear what you want. It must be so embarrassing, and make you feel inferior to rich kids in their designer stuff. Big smile time.

'Officer Hackness!'

'Sally, you look as radiant as ever!'

'I am not, Officer Hackness. Look, what do you make of this notice they put on my desk?'

'Sounds to me like your bosses are looking after you!'

'Well, I guess you don't need one at the station. You can just arrest anyone who is abusive!'

Oh shit, I should not have said that. I sense a lecture coming on.

'Well, Sally, it's not like that…'

Phew, a guest, just in time.

'I am so sorry, but I must deal with this guest.'

'Of course.'

'Oh, don't worry about me, police work is very important. Holds the fabric of society together. Where would we be without them?'

No, please don't encourage him!

'Thank you for saying that, it's nice to be appreciated once in a while. But I must go have my coffee, police work never stops.'

*

Looks like my single mum is taking Lily out for the day. Oh, Lily is coming over here, how nice.

'Hello, Lily!'

'Hello, flowers!'

Ignore me, then.

'Flowers, today I am going to the zoo. I'll see all the animals and have an ice cream. I'll tell you all about it later!'

Oh, that it? Off she goes. At least I got a little smile from her before she ran off. Seems good old Sally is of less interest than the flowers! Somehow she reminds me of myself. I spent a lot of time alone as a girl. I wonder if a single child misses having a brother or sister? Going to the zoo will be nice. It's not a big one, but there is little in the city apart from shopping for kids to do during the day. It must be hard for parents to bring kids up in cities. No wonder children end up hanging around in the shopping mall.

*

Here comes a guest with the 'whinger look'. It's the one where they look as if they're in pain, like something in their life is torturing them. Sometimes whingers smile, but it's a pained smile. It must be hard, living a life of misery. But whingers probably like that.

'Good morning, how can I help you?'

'Mr Wilson, room 1308.'

Oh yes, Matt warned me about him. So, how do I handle this? I'm supposed to ask, 'How was your stay?' But if I do, he'll probably think I am taking the piss. He'll want to whinge so I might as well give him the chance to let off a bit of steam before I try to get him focused. But he may go on and on. Dilemma time. I'll just look at the screen and type away. He's not saying anything yet.

'Here are your room charges, please check them carefully.'

I am sure he will. He'll query something – he must.

'That's fine. Here's my card.'

What? He's not going to moan about anything?

'Hope to see you again soon.'

No reply, and off he goes. How come he hasn't whinged? He had to change room twice and complained about pretty much everything. Why did he say nothing? Is he all whinged out? I can't believe it!

'Flowers, what do you make of that?'

I can only assume that he'll be seeking a refund from Mr Temple directly. I guess he may think that if he gets a deal from me it won't be good enough. I hate whingers, although they are the ones I have to appear to be nicest to. Well, actually it's more about looking understanding than being nice. Faking a concerned, understanding expression goes a long way in this business! I am allowed a little flexibility to do a 'whinger deal', make them think they are compensated. The trick is to make them think they have got something for nothing, or have succeeded in being overcompensated. Anything major and I have to get my supervisor Frank to authorise it, but he is never around when needed, and never answers his phone. I can't win with whinger deals. If I do them without his permission I get told off, and yet if I let the guest leave without one, and they moan to management later, or write a bad review online, I also get told off. I don't understand the mentality of major whingers. Some minor

36

whinger types are just looking for something for nothing – an upgrade, a free dessert in the restaurant, that kind of thing. But 'Whinger of the Day' candidates have a negative attitude towards everything in life. Surely it can't be fun. They are miserable and stay that way, even though they're usually well off financially. Don't they want to be happy?

To make dealing with complaints more fun, I play a game. I try and spot who will be tomorrow's Whinger of the Day. I try and guess who will be the worst at check-out. Then, when the person is really shitty with me, I don't mind if it's the person I guessed! I almost want them to be a super-whinger! I can usually tell a likely Whinger of the Day the moment they arrive. One sign is if they take a mint from my bowl without asking. That's plain rude, isn't it? A real big-time potential whinger will take more than one mint. It's a good test on check-in. As I see it, taking mints without asking is impolite. I always give mint stealers one of our poorer rooms – next to the lift shaft is my favourite punishment! They are going to whinge anyway, there's no point wasting a lovely room on them. Let someone who will appreciate it have it, I say!

In particular, I really hope guests don't have an evening meal and breakfast included in the room rate. They will whinge about the limited set menu, looking for a discount. My attitude is that hotels should never offer packages that include meals. It only encourages whingers. Maybe they should stay in a cheaper hotel if they cannot afford to pay full price for the food. Anyway, why would anyone eat in a hotel restaurant when the city has a great selection of nicer and cheaper places to dine in?

Some people are not really whingers, they just don't understand how hotels work. For example, you can tell the difference between someone who has travelled and someone who has not. People get confused over the pre-authorisation of their cards, or why their room is not available before check-in time. Those who have never travelled abroad can be the worst complainers: 'It's not like we are used to at home.' Of course it's not, not everyone does things like you, that's the point of travel!

*

Oh, this guy's a bit casually dressed. In work boots, I'm not used to guests looking like that!

'Good morning, how can I help you?'

Don't put those grubby fingers on my desk, and no, you'd better not try helping yourself to a mint with those hands.

'It's me, Bill.'

Who on earth is Bill? He looks to be in his middle fifties, a bit overweight – I bet he drinks beer. You couldn't drink wine with hands like that. I don't recognise the face, am I supposed to? I hate not remembering names, but there is only one Sally and a hundred guests who change all the time so I can be forgiven the occasional mistake, surely? I am so embarrassed. What do I say? Only one thing to do: smile.

'Bill!'

'Sorry I'm late, I've had my hands full this morning, but I'm all yours now, sweetheart!'

Late? Did I have an appointment with him? What gives him the right to call me 'sweetheart'? Maybe he has the wrong person, but there is only me at reception. Maybe he thinks I'm Katie from the evening shift. Now, what do I say next without making myself look stupid? He looks a bit like one of the guys from the DIY store. Did I ask him to come see me at reception? No, I'd never do that. I hope I am not looking too confused.

'The mirror, you said it wobbled?'

Oh, phew! It's the maintenance guy! I was thinking it was someone important – well, you know what I mean. So, he's called Bill, I don't ever remember meeting him. He must be new.

'Yes, it's wobbling when the lobby doors open, it's the breeze.'

'OK.'

Off he trots, well, waddles is more like it.

'Flowers, look at what he's doing!'

He's shaking it! If it's loose it'll come crashing down on him! That's it, he's coming back. No doubt with an experienced eye and his scientific method he will come to some startling conclusion!

'It's OK. It was never fitted tight to the wall, but it's secure.'

'So it doesn't need tightening?'

'No, see you.'

Off he waddles. Where do they get them from?

*

Aha, here's Ed the courier, right on schedule. He'd probably be proud if I told him he was 'on schedule'. Guess that's the kind of thing delivery people get off on.

'Here comes Santa.'

'Why do you keep calling me Santa?'

'Because you keep turning up at my desk with parcels!'

I know why he comes to the reception desk when he should go to the office. Coming here is an excuse to chat me up.

'One may be addressed to you one day!'

A gift for me? Ha! I feel lonely enough sometimes, no need to dig it in.

'What's your excuse this time for bothering me rather than the office?'

'There's nobody in the office, and this needs signing for.'

'They are probably AWOL with the managers. I haven't seen Frank all morning, but he is around, apparently!'

'What's this on the desk? You won a certificate?'

You are right, it's on my desk and shouldn't be there. I think that's the first time you have ever noticed anything about me or my desk. You are normally so full of yourself.

'No, it's a stupid notice Mr Temple has insisted I have on the desk!'

'Let's see. Why's it behind the mints? It makes it hard to read. Oh, what a shame, I'm not allowed to abuse you! Bet you would love me to!'

Groan. No, you are still the same jerk. That's just the puerile type of comment I expect the sign to lead to, especially from a juvenile like you.

'So when do I get to take you out for a drink after work?'

You are nice, but too young. Fun, yes, you seem it, but I reckon you are boring once at home. I can imagine you

40

play computer games all night, with online so-called friends you have never met. Maybe you'll watch sport on TV, but really only pretending you are interested, so you can say you 'watched the game' when chatting to work associates or customers. I'm too tired for the bar scene after work. As a special treat, yes, but with you it would be out all weekend until you have spent your credit card limit.

'As always, never. Find someone your own age.'

Cute, fit body though.

Oh bugger, it's Mr Temple. Why is Frank never here when the boss is around?

'Where's the RDM?'

'What?'

'The RDM.'

Please stop this management textbook shit.

'Do you mean Frank?'

'Yes, the RDM.'

So why the hell didn't you just say Frank?

'No idea.'

'Tell him I need to see him ASAP.'

I feel my stomach dropping. Maybe I'm in the shit over the sign.

'OK.'

Plonker. RDM: rostered duty manager. Frank's more of a ruddy desertion manager.

'Well, flowers, there we are. I knew the notice would cause trouble!'

Did you hear what Ed the courier said? He thinks I would love to be abused by him. What a dickhead. Like Mr Temple. All this management course crap is making me feel bullied, degraded and generally seriously pissed off. Not that I can do anything about it. Good old Sally just has to take it.

*

Good grief. Cheesy smiles from people in slightly dated clothing. Who the hell are they? They remind me of the religious types from my childhood – probably coming to save me!

'Good morning! How can I help you?'

'Hello, we are looking for Daniel Akkad, we believe he is staying here.'

'Let me have a look on the system.'

I don't like these people, there's something about them.

'There's nobody of that name staying here, I am afraid. Do you have a room number?'

'No.'

He's not checked in, nor is he on the system as due to arrive. I wonder why they think he is here? Probably the wrong hotel.

'In that case I'm afraid I can't really do much more. Would you like to leave a message in case he does arrive? Reservations are not always made in the name of the occupant.'

'Oh, we were sure he was staying here.'

'I'm sorry I can't be more help. Are you sure you won't leave a message?'

'No, maybe we'll come back later.'

Cheesy goodbye smile. Hmm. That was strange. I wonder who they were? They didn't even leave a leaflet,

I'm sure they are religious. Especially the woman – an old-fashioned flowery dress, and the colours! They are as bad as any mixed bunch! She should have got one with colours that go together. I mean, pink and green are a big no-no: girlie and jealous, that surely does not go. Why's that guy by the bar staring at them? Oh, he's coming over here.

'Hi, those two people who were just here, what did they want?'

I wish I knew, it's a bit strange.

'I'm sorry but I cannot tell you, guest confidentiality. By the way, don't I know you?'

'My name is Brandon. Haven't we seen each other around town? I go to the bar in the mall.'

A lot, I think you forgot to add. Just because I might recognise you, it won't make me tell.

'What are you doing here?'

'Oh no, I cannot possibly tell you. Client confidentiality. Now I have got to go.'

'Touché.'

Nice guy. I bet he's a private detective. He doesn't look like one, and stinks of alcohol. Mind you, some of the most famous detectives on TV and in films drink. You cannot always tell what someone does for a living. Like that guy Andrew who came in the other day. Tourist T-shirt, stained shorts, unshaven, red-faced, stinking of beer. Said he used to be a stockbroker, and was now a writer and wanted to chat with me about life at reception, as if! But you never know!

*

43

OK, OK, phone, I'm coming! I am sure you are flashing more vigorously than usual, can you sense the urgency of the caller?

'Good morning, Ms Wilks, Sally at reception speaking, how can I help you?'

'It's Miss Wilks. I've been trying to get through to room service but nobody is answering.'

I'm not surprised. Poor Peter the barman has been hassled by you ever since you checked in yesterday. I'm sure he ignored you when he saw the number flash up, he's about half your age.

'I am sorry, Miss Wilks, can I take your order?'

'I am one of those people who are happy to be called Miss. I want no doubt about my single status. I am a free woman, and still very young at heart! Ms makes me sound divorced. I am not, I just haven't found a guy rich enough to marry yet!'

She's paused. Am I supposed to comment? Do I laugh or sympathise? I feel like I am talking to Miss Wilks the headmistress, and am supposed to give the correct answer. At least she is on the phone. If she could see me now, I have the expression of a confused rabbit in the glare of car headlights! What's the answer? I can imagine her being handy with a cane across the hands or buttocks if I get it wrong! I wonder what expression she is making? Probably glee at the idea of giving me a good whack!

'I would like a bottle of Chardonnay from the bar.'

Phew! Sometimes saying nothing is best.

'No problem, and how many glasses would you like with that?'

'Oh, just one – no, let me think… no, two.'

You won't get lucky, the barman's still a while from his lunch break!

'OK, I'll get that sorted out for you right away. It shouldn't take too long.'

'Thank you. Oh, and if Peter the barman can bring some of those hot roasted nuts too.'

Oh, it's Peter is it – you're now on first name terms? Sorry, sweetheart, you may know his name by now, but I reckon this will be a waitress from the kitchen, he is far too busy making coffee for you.

'I'm sure we can find you some hot nuts.'

Did I really say that? Tut, tut!

'Thank you.'

She didn't get it, or ignored it.

*

Come on, Frank, it's time for my lunch break and I need the toilet! Oh bugger. Another person coming to the desk with a cheesy smile and I'm desperate to pee! Damn you, Frank.

'Good morning! How can I help you?'

'My name is Shedfield, John Shedfield. I have a reservation for tonight.'

'I'm afraid check-in starts at 2pm.'

Please say that's OK and piss off, I need to wee!

'I know, but please can I have a room now, any room? I need to change for lunch.'

All I want is to pee. It's his lucky day. I cannot be faffing around, I need to pee. Sally, just click on the first free room.

'Let me see. OK.'

'Thank you. Let me return the favour and invite you to join me for dinner!'

'Could I have your credit card please? I need to pre-authorise it for incidentals.'

And that does not include me.

'Dinner?'

'Sorry, company policy doesn't allow staff to socialise with the guests – no mixing business and pleasure.'

And I don't do 'business' for one lousy free meal!

'Think about it.'

I did, and said no. Please go away, I am in agony!

'The lifts are that way.'

Frank!

CHAPTER 3

LUNCHTIME!

'It's time for lunch, flowers!'

What a crappy morning. I feel bullied by Mr Temple, insisting the notice stays on our desk. I think he thinks I am stronger than I am. I really don't want it there, it's too much stress. At least my chat-up statistics are looking good! The men like Ed the courier and that boat guy John. I don't mind getting chatted up. In fact I quite like the idea that somebody wants me, in whatever way. But just because I am alone, it does not mean I am desperate for sex. Sex is not the main thing, I love my little egg vibrator and enjoy my romantic films at home. It's the company I am looking for, but I'm used to being alone, happy enough in my world. Everyone has faults, and the ones that I get here certainly have. The roses in a coffin from the guy in the brown suit – I mean, how not to impress a lady! At least it's easy for me to politely reject them. I am at work, and in this job there are standard excuses I can use. That helps me feel in control. Talking to strangers socially is difficult for me. No problem at work, but when I have to make small talk I find it boring, and don't know what to say.

'Flowers, today is a sushi day.'

I like the type of people who buy sushi. They are posh office workers in suits and smart clothes. Although it's a bit expensive for me, I join the line and feel like one of them. It's a real treat, and I deserve one after the way I have suffered this morning! Maybe I should have been a secretary, but think I couldn't cope with the close personal work. I like my desk between me and others.

'See you after lunch!'

A quick look in the mirror. Hmm, presentable, but it's not a red-and-black checked ribbon day after all. I was wrongly got at by Mr Temple over the notice. Inside me there is a little girl that wants to pout, but she can't come out. I'm unable to feel like I want to when dressed like this. I need a dash of cute, girlie pink. No time to change my red nail polish so it will have to be pink panties. I'll need to change the ribbon to red-and-pink checks too. Better go get them now.

*

What do you think, mirror? That looks perfect. A nice red-and-pink checked ribbon, in a perfect bow. Teeth brushed, make-up restored, nothing stuck to teeth, no stains on clothing. Good. Here we go, only four hours and I'm out of here. What a sweet girlie I am now! Yes, it's definitely a red-and-pink checked bow type of afternoon!

'Hi, flowers, I'm back! But what's the matter with you?'

Who's been messing with you? I bet that irritating florist has deliberately come and changed some of you while I was at lunch! She hasn't a clue how to arrange flowers. I have to

48

rearrange you every time she passes by, don't I? How many times have I said to her, 'No yellow flowers. I like reds for passion and pinks for girlishness in the vase!' They suit my personality and match my nails, lipstick and phone covers. I don't mind purple flowers, they are sophisticated and purple is a royal colour. But yellow doesn't go with anything on the desk. I wear a black suit, so the desk would look like an unwelcoming wasp if I had yellow flowers! So, yellow rose, I'll have to give you to the office. They'll like you there, they are their own little clique, and yellow flowers mean friendship. Yellow also means irresponsible, so there we go, perfect!

'So, flowers, notice the change in bow?'

I have pink panties on! Shame only Mr Temple may notice. His security cameras behind the desk catch everything! I need to hitch up my skirt when I crouch down to get to the lower drawer. I wonder if, after all this time, he has decoded my ribbon patterns? If so, he will know what a nice girlie I am in pink panties and remove that nasty notice from our desk!

CHAPTER 4

GOOD AFTERNOON!

Look what just came in through the lobby doors. Here she comes, Mrs Designer Label. She must be a Mrs as nobody would buy all that with their own money. Bow-wow. Nice handbag though.

'Good…'

'I have a reservation, the little man I spoke to assured me I'll be on the top floor.'

What, how rude, interrupting me like that, and did she just say little man?! Jack in reservations is rumoured to be well endowed!

'What name is the booking under?'

'Smith.'

Aha! Whenever anyone checks in under the name Smith it gives them an air of mystery! Although it's a common name, I always wonder if it's false or not!

'Let's see.'

What? No way is she having 1809, it's the corner suite with double aspect. Not at that rate. Jack is such a sucker for a posh tart! Time for the pained smile.

'I am afraid that whilst requests can be made, we cannot guarantee them. The top floor is very popular, and unfortunately there is no availability. I can give you a twin aspect room on the second floor.'

As an added luxury, you get the smell and noise from the restaurant too.

'But the man said…'

Oh, he is a bit bigger now, is he?

'Well, there is a suite available on that floor, but it's three times the room rate.'

'Oh, no.'

Will she crack and pay, scream for the manager or go for it?

'I want a view.'

'Room 1405 has a nice view.'

And is next to the lift shaft. *Burr, click, burr, click!*

'OK, I'll take that.'

And are you going to ask for a discount? Silence – no.

'How would you like to pay?'

'By card.'

What on earth is she doing? It's a dog! How the hell did I not notice that in her handbag? She's putting the little runt on my desk. Get the damned thing off!

'Aw, isn't she cute, she's shaking.'

'You're a boy, aren't you, Pooie?'

I'd shake if I had to be with her 24/7.

'I'm sorry, madam, we are a small pet friendly hotel, but we have a bowl of sweets here that guests eat, so for health and safety regulations the dog will have to go on the floor.'

Where it may get trodden on and put out of its misery.

'We can't let poor Pooipoos stand on that cold marble, can we?'

Ooh, a nice designer purse out of a nice designer handbag, with nice designer dog hair on it. Or is it? No, it's a fake bag – the logo is not quite as it should be!

'That's a nice handbag.'

'My husband brought it back for me from Italy.'

And she didn't notice? He obviously got it from some knock-off street trader. At least if the dog pisses in it it's a fake one!

'That's nice, I've never been to Italy. In fact I've never been abroad, I am embarrassed to say.'

'Oh, you must travel. It's a wonderful experience, we do it all the time. You learn so much about life. I have to admit that sometimes it's hard work, but well worth the effort. Afterwards it's always nice to get back home again.'

Out comes the credit card – grey. I think it's funny how people get fussy over the colour of their cards. Platinum and silver both look the same to me, so they are not a good status symbol. Green, black or red cards mean nothing, like you are not one end of the spectrum or the other. A sort of middle-class card, the owner not rich enough for something better. Only gold is gold – even if almost anyone can have one these days, it has to be the colour to have!

'I do like your bow! You don't see women in bows much these days, but I think they are so nice. Much more feminine than the elastic band things everyone uses now.'

Is she calling me old-fashioned? I bloody hope not!

'How nice of you to say that. There is a store in the street at the back of the hotel, they have ribbon, although these days it's hard to find a good selection. You can get ribbon on the Internet, even your own design. But I like the shop, the atmosphere in it. It's sort of cosy, and the woman running it is so chatty and interested in what you want.'

'Thank you for that, I may pop in to see.'

'Here's your key, have a nice stay.'

'Did you see that, flowers?'

How dare she put that excuse for a dog on our desk? The thing was shaking like a leaf! I'm not surprised, carried around in that cheapo bag. What kind of person has a dog like that? At the animal sanctuary all the animals are taken proper care of. That's why I like to go there. They have all had sad lives, but at least they can rest, recover in peace. I wish I could. I'd better call and have a word with Jack in reservations about the room.

'Jack, it's Sally at reception.'

Every time I call him I think about how well-endowed he is supposed to be. I can't get his genitals out of my head when talking to him. It's like they are talking to me!

'Hi, Sally, what can I do for you?'

'You put a Mrs Smith in the suite, but her room rate wasn't correct.'

'Let me have a look… Smith, no, it's a typo, it should be Smithson. It's for some guy, he was very insistent so I was able to get him to pay the full rate.'

'Oh, it's a good job I didn't put her in there then. She seemed to think she would be in a special room.'

'I'm not sure who she is. We get a lot of people calling because they want to see if there is a better rate than the one on the Internet, even though it says our best rate is on our website. They think by talking to me there is still room for an upgrade or a bit extra off!'

If a woman charms you with a posh voice, there obviously is.

'You'd never do that, would you?'

'Of course not.'

Lying bugger. No harm trying to improve your booking by calling if you can be bothered. Especially as you need to navigate about ten different options on the phone – the last is to hold on to actually speak to someone. At least the music they play while you're waiting is not selected by the boss! Reservations do make mistakes, but never seem to learn from them. They cause so many problems with the wrong room types, the dates messed up etc. I know sometimes it's the guest's fault for not explaining clearly what they want, or not listening properly to what they are told. But I am sure that being sat in that little room staring at the screen all day must be bad for one's concentration.

*

There goes Mr Shedfield, all spruced up for lunch. I wonder who he's going to try and chat up next? He'll probably start in a bar with some unsuspecting barmaid. He'll annoy her until he's bored because she is not taking the bait. Then he'll wander off to a restaurant and pester a waitress whilst having his lunch. She'll start polite and chatty, even though she'll be able to tell he's half pissed from the bar, hoping for a good tip. I imagine he'll keep attempting to chat to her whilst she is trying to serve other people and piss her off. Just like me at reception, bar and restaurant workers are being polite to you, it doesn't mean they like you. Why customers don't get that

I'll never know. We are not fair game in a reality TV dating programme! I know some people don't get out much, or are shy, so some contact with other people is better than nothing, and nice. I understand some lonely pensioners go shopping every day just to get some contact with other people. That's fine, living alone I get that one. But just because we deal with the public does not mean you can hit on us to the point of annoyance. Well, not unless I wanted you to chat me up. The trouble is, how can I signal the difference between being polite and actually interested? How do I avoid looking too keen or desperate, or like an easy lay?

What do you think, mirror? Am I attractive today? Hmm, I guess there's always room for improvement. Oh shit, Mr Shedfield saw me staring at you. Bugger, he's coming over here, with his cheesy smile at full stretch!

'Hello, Mr Shedfield, how can I help you?'

'You remembered me, how thoughtful…'

'It's my job.'

'…Sally.'

'You remembered me too, I see, how thoughtful!'

He read my badge – an excuse to enjoy a stare at my cleavage too, no doubt.

'It's my job. I'm guest relations manager on the cruise ship that's leaving in a couple of days.'

'Do people call you the GRM?'

'What? No, of course not!'

'You would be here! Mr Temple, the boss, would demand that I tell him where the GRM was!' In your case, that would be a generally retarded male. 'He's responsible for this notice on the desk. Do you have one?'

'I think somewhere on the boat there is something like that. But it's hard to find, on a wall where people don't hang around much. We don't want people thinking we have abusive guests! Everyone has to be happy on the boat – that's the job of my team, to make sure!'

Oh, 'my team', is it? Uff, what a big-headed git. Just like Mr Temple.

'I noticed you have changed your bow, Sally.'

Why does he keep using my name? Maybe to help himself remember it? Probably just like Mr Temple, a technique straight from a management course on how to be a GRM!

'Yes, I decided it was a red-and-pink checked ribbon day today.'

I hope I'm not blushing. He'll be wondering what that means… I sort of hope. Did I just think that? Oh no, surely not!

'And what exactly is a red-and-pink checked ribbon day?'

It's for you to find out. Maybe. But not today. Not with a check pattern.

'It's a female thing.'

'I prefer spots, actually.'

You probably would, if you knew what that meant. However, I reckon stripes are more your style.

'I board the ship tomorrow, so tonight's my last night on dry land for a while. Where do you recommend I take you to dinner?'

'I'm afraid I am busy tonight, but have a nice lunch. I have people waiting to check in.'

'See you later!'

Not if I can help it.

'Flowers, did you hear that?!'

He noticed my ribbon had changed! How sweet. Mind you, working on a cruise ship doesn't impress. Who wants a partner who's never at home, and probably shagging any bit of skirt he can get? On the other hand, not having him around all the time probably has some advantages!

*

Oops, didn't see the phone light flashing.

'Sally at reception, how can I help?'

'It's Maria.'

Groan – what's she wanting to dump on me now? I am busy.

'Maria, what's the problem?'

'When I call you always seem to think there's a problem!'

There is, she never calls when there isn't a problem.

'There usually is!'

'The guests in 1507 have taken the towels from the room.'

'You sure they didn't take them to the pool and leave them there?'

'Guests know they must not use room towels by the pool. There are towels for that purpose at the gym.'

'Yes, but some people don't want to walk through the hotel in their swimming costumes, so tend to wrap a towel around themselves. Also, with the air conditioning here they'd probably freeze to death!'

'Anyway, they took the face cloths too, and the hand towels!'

'OK, in that case you are right. I'll charge it to their card as a supplemental. By the way, have you met the new maintenance guy?'

'Bill? Yes, but he's not new, he's been here at least a month. I reckon he just tries to avoid working. Never answers his phone, but we all know that trick!'

'OK, thanks.'

How come Maria knew he was called Bill, and how come I don't recognise him or know his name after one month? It's like a family for me here. Discovering Bill is bit like finding a relative you never knew you had!

'Flowers, I hate having to do supplemental charges.'

The guest will call accounts and complain about the incorrect billing. Accounts will then call me and accuse me of incorrect billing. I'll have forgotten what it was about and have to look it up on the system.

They will say the customer, not guest, is on the line and holding. I'll say, 'Make them wait.' Accounts will tell me to hurry up, they have a job to do. I'll say, 'So do I', and then that they took the towels. Accounts will suggest they are put through to me, so I get the shit to deal with. It'll be 'No we didn't', 'Yes you did' for about two minutes. Then they'll threaten to talk to the boss, as if I should be terrified. I'll offer to put them through. Somewhere in the process, hopefully, they'll hang up!

*

'Mr Charles, how lovely to see you again!'

'Hello, Sally, yes, my company keep sending me to see you!'

He's not going to think it's lovely when I tell him he can't have his favourite room. I didn't realise he was coming today – he requested 1809 but that is already allocated. Shit, I know he really doesn't handle change very well. He seems to be a very routine-led guy. Organised to the point of tediousness.

'I'm afraid your usual room is taken. I am so sorry.' Time to put on a pained expression, then pull a face at the screen, then smile. It must look and sound really fake, but it works. 'Although we are really busy, I can fit you on our top floor today. Room 1803 is free but there's no corner view, I am afraid.'

Wait for him to be a pain…

'I like double aspect rooms, do you have one on the fourth floor?'

What? Why does he want to be on the fourth floor? What's that all about?

'Let me see… yes, 1407 is available, and ready now.'

I don't get it. He is so fixed in his ways, he didn't even make that boohooing expression he thinks is funny. Mind you, both rooms have basically the same layout.

'Thank you, I'll take that. Don't forget my loyalty card number.'

'It's in the system as always, Mr Charles!'

I've got to find out more. He's up to something. Why the fourth floor? Why not a higher one, the seventh for example?

'So, what brings you into town today?'

'To see you again, of course! You know how precious you are to me.'

Precious? Don't even go there, I know you are married, you were here with your wife last month! And don't try the crap about how she doesn't understand you. I've also had it with management training courses, especially the ones on how to motivate your staff by faking being nice to them. What good do they do? As a result of them I have a stupid notice spoiling my desk, I have a boss who has swapped names for initials, and a guy who was trained to think it will motivate me to help him if he uses words like 'precious'! I am sure he saves 'valuable', 'wanted' and 'needed' for his bloody loyalty points!

'The company are having their quarterly meeting tomorrow, so I have to present my results.'

Yes, he's in his usual suit. In fact, I think I have never seen him in anything but that – oh, and his polo shirt he wears later in the evening, the same one every time. Well, maybe he doesn't just have one, maybe he always wears the same style. Actually, thinking about it, his suit is the same design but looks newer. I guess he has a store loyalty card as well as a hotel one. Yes, I can imagine that he likes checking how many points he has on each card. He must shit himself if any are due to expire! No, he will know exactly when and schedule a stay or shop months in advance.

'That's good. Your results OK?'

'Impressive, Sally, impressive.'

You are supposed to end that sentence with 'although I

say it myself'. Mr Charles is not full of shit, he just comes across as a bit of a jerk.

'I am pleased to hear it. Here's your room key.'

Please don't try to treat me like a personal secretary this time. Don't say I'd make a great secretary, how I'd be better than yours. I bet she hates him, deep down. I know you mainly do it as an excuse to chat to me. A guest service agent – sorry, GSA – is not a guest secretarial agent, and I can be a generally stupid arsehole if you get on the wrong side of me!

*

Now, two guys, no laptop or business cases, smart casual dress. Obviously not businessmen.

'Good afternoon! How can I help you?'

'We have a reservation, here's the booking.'

'Let me see. Yes, a king bed room for two nights.'

Now I need to pause the conversation, I must try to look busy, give them a chance to say something in case that's wrong.

'What's the background music? It's a fun selection, reminds me of our misspent youth in discos!'

Don't tell me they like the manager's selection. How disappointing.

'It's the manager's choice. I have to listen to it all day, every day. It's not fun for me!'

They did not say twin bed room, so all clear.

'Here are your keys. Let me know if I can be of any more help. Have a nice stay with us!'

That went well. There's nothing more embarrassing than having to ask if people of the same sex want separate beds.

*

There goes Mrs Smith, off out with her bag. I assume she's taking Pooipoos for 'walkies'. He'll probably get exhausted, I imagine he'll shake all the way round the park! I wonder if she has little designer bags for his poo? I cannot imagine her actually picking up his shit at all – surely that's not her style! But look at her change of clothes. She was dressed smart but dull when she arrived. Now she's in quite a colourful outfit!

*

Here we go. Fat, sweaty kid rushing to the desk before his parents can get through the lobby door with their cases. I bet he wants the Wi-Fi code.

'What's the room number, what's the room number? I need it for the Wi-Fi!'

Who do you think you are, screaming at me like that? You rude so-and-so. I don't like your attitude, and although I could give you it, I won't.

'You can't use it until you are checked in, it won't take a minute. Here come your parents.'

'We have a reservation for one night, we are the Whites. What's the matter, son?'

'The lady won't let me have the room number.'

What? He's threatening to cry!

'I just need you to sign here and here and then he can have access to the Internet.'

I don't believe it, tears over Wi-Fi! What happened to crying from fear or pain? Not bloody Wi-Fi, surely.

'Now look what you have done! Poor thing – just one second, son. You keep moving, think calories and kilometres!'

I reckon he cried because he couldn't have his own way. What a spoilt brat!

'Are you exercising?'

Dieting is what he needs, not just exercise!

'I have a fitness tracker, look! It measures all the calories I burn off in a day. I can print out a chart of it too!'

At least it's stopped him boohooing. Distracting young children who are upset is a tactic normally used for babies, but this kid is a teenager!

'That's impressive!'

Not only did I lie, I smiled too. Isn't Sally a nice lady, eh? At least I can appear nice and he won't try to chat me up!

'It measures everything I do.'

I guess bugger all most of the time. It's calories in, not out that's your problem, matey. You should be out playing sport with your friends, if you have any, which I suspect you don't. I'll give you some exercise, you spoilt brat. Let's change room 1206 up a bit.

'You are in room 1807. It's a lovely top-floor room.' And next to the lift shaft. *Burr, click, burr, click*. 'The lifts are over there, and the stairs are next to them – it's eight floors up if he wants to burn off a bit more!'

'What do you mean, burn off a bit more? A bit more what?'

Oh no. It's the politically correct brigade!

'Calories.'

'You meant F-A-T, didn't you? You are not allowed to use that word, it's derogative and insulting. It hurts his feelings and that is brutality. We'll have to speak to your boss about this, but we have to get moving.'

'Mummy, did she use the naughty word, the one that's never to be spoken?'

'No, son, but she was thinking it and that's just as bad.'

I assume he is an only child. I can't imagine anyone wanting another after that. Waddle off. Bet you take the lift. Yes you did, eight floors too much for you, eh? I thought so.

*

Here comes Mr Temple again, but this time he is not looking around. He's looking straight at me. Oh shit. Is he still pissed off about the notice? Maybe he realises I've changed my panties. Am I blushing? I'd better cut him off before he starts talking.

'Mr Temple, about the notice—'

'It stays.'

Bastard. How can girlie pink fail? It worked on John – mind you, anything probably would!

'A guest who is a manager on a cruise ship tells me they have a notice like that.'

'Of course, we all care about our staff.'

Lying toad.

'He says that it gives the wrong impression. It makes it sound like you have guests who are rough and abusive. Not

64

the image you want to portray. They have their notice on the wall.'

Anything other than my desk, please, please.

'People wouldn't read it if it wasn't in their faces. How many people really look at the fire escape plan on the back of their room doors and memorise the escape route? Very few! All GSAs need to go to the PDR to do their PDR and KPIs with HR on a JIT basis.'

What on earth is he on about?

'Sorry?'

'HR need to meet you.'

'OK, I'll call them.'

'ASAP.'

'ASAP!'

Sir. Shouldn't I salute at this point?

'So, flowers, should I have saluted?'

The younger staff here are happy with his style. They have all attended hospitality training courses at college. I had to learn my job as I went along. But the young staff are all terribly professional about their careers. I have a job, my only job for many years. No career for good old Sally, just a job for me until I retire. No need to learn GSA or GSM shit. I'm sure they talk that crap just to sound terribly professional. They probably don't even remember what most of it means. Half the time they don't use them correctly and look stupid. What's wrong with names anyway? Aren't we humans, not machines?

*

'Flowers, if it isn't Miss Wilks heading to the bar!'

She must have finished her Chardonnay quickly! Maybe she only had a glass after discovering Peter didn't bring it to her room. She is such a predator. She dresses provocatively but, until now, with a bit of class. She's in a see-though blouse with a sexy bra. Her colours are more strident than yesterday, she's obviously getting more desperate. I wonder what she does for a living?

'Oh, look, flowers, Mr Charles is going to the bar.'

Poor thing, there is a big bad wolf lying in wait! She'll talk to him as soon as he has his drink served. She'll whinge about the service if she's not getting the attention she wants from Peter! I am sure she is good at breaking the ice in conversation with strangers, a professional at it. Now, let's see what she does for work. No, she has nothing down on her record for occupation. I wish people would say, it sometimes helps, especially if I am feeling nosy.

*

Phew, something stinks. What is that sweaty smell? Not me, I haven't even farted.

'Hello.'

Oh, it's a guest. I hope he didn't see me pull a face.

'Good afternoon, how can I help you?'

He is really smelly. Where did I leave the air freshener spray? We should get a permanent one for around here.

'I'd like to check in – the name is Green.'

I hope he can't tell I am going to start coughing.

'Let me see.'

I'm gagging, he must be just off a very long flight.

'Travelled far?'

'No, moving hotel.'

I so want to ask if there was a problem with the water, but I guess they threw you out!

'Oh, why?'

'They couldn't extend my stay as they were fully booked!'

Are you sure they didn't want you stinking the place out?

'Here you are, room 1205. The stairs are just there by the lift, they'll be quicker.'

Oh no, the lift's opening. Shit, he's getting in. So is another guest. I can see her looking around as if to say, 'Where did that smell come from?' Hurry up, get in the lift, I need to spray! I hope my clothes don't stink. I visited a pig farm once and my clothes reeked afterwards. I feel sorry for the next person who gets in the lift, maybe I should go spray in there too.

'You OK, flowers?'

Not wilting under the stench? I was – wasn't he a smelly guy? At least you smell nice. Well, unless the florist is too lazy to change your water, but I make sure you stay fresh. People should shower before going out in public, and put on fresh clothes. These days, with modern deodorants, there is no excuse for smelling. It's inconsiderate and antisocial. Why do some people let themselves get so smelly? You would think they'd have more self-respect. It's not fair on everybody else. But the politically correct say you cannot mention smells. It's probably classified as bullying! Well, I feel bullied when they force their stink on me. It's like nasal rape!

'Good afternoon, Mr Hill, nice to see you again!'

'Err, yes.'

Poor Mr Hill. He always looks so nervous when he comes to stay here. He'll start sweating soon, he usually does.

'I have you in the same room as last time, you said how much you liked it.'

'Err, yes, I did, didn't I? Can't think why. Oh, shouldn't have said that. Don't know what you might think. No, that's not what I mean. Oh dear.'

'I can change the room if you want?'

'Oh no, it's fine.'

'So, what brings you into town this time?'

Please say something – it takes a minute to do the paperwork, but it'll feel like an age if you don't talk. Even if you are too shy to look directly at me, please don't gaze at the floor, that makes me feel like I am too ugly to look at!

'Err, the usual meetings.'

Now he's blushing. Is it talking to me that causes it? Why is he like this?

'There we go, here is your key and do have a nice stay with us!'

'Oh, thank you.'

Toddle off. You are forty-five, yet remind me more of an old man than a shy kid.

'Flowers, how the hell he became a sales manager I have no idea!'

Of course, maybe he wasn't always like that. Maybe something happened to change him. I wonder what.

CHAPTER 5

CHECKING IN?

Well, well. The Wilks has caught its prey. Mr Charles is heading out with her. I bet he's invited her to lunch, and is pleased with himself for getting the date. In fact, he is flirting with her a bit, but look – he doesn't care that his oh-so-precious Sally can see him. Maybe in his screwed-up male mind he thinks I'll be jealous and want him more. Some women might – idiots. Why can't men see that women are often in control? They just do it more subtly! Mind you, in this case, Miss Wilks may be very unsubtle with him. I am sure he will appreciate her firm headmistress style manner. The cane will be out if he doesn't recite his ten times table correctly! It'll be interesting to see where this leads – I hope at least one of them is back before the end of my shift. They could just be friendly – why do I always assume it's about sex? It frequently is, but this is a little odd.

Peter the barman is looking a little furtive. Why's he walking over here looking like he's sneaking through a jungle on the lookout for tigers?

'Is it safe to come out yet?'

'Oh, you just saw Miss Wilks and Mr Charles leave.'

'Yes, here's your espresso macchiato!'

I love the sound of those words. They transport me to Italy. I could be in a hotel there right now.

'She wanted room service from you earlier.'

'I know, fortunately I managed to get one of the kitchen staff to deal with it. Apparently when the door opened she was in some fancy underwear, she must have thought I was bringing it up! She was probably hoping to catch me just before my break!'

Silly bitch.

'She will have been so disappointed! I hope she hasn't got it in for you now. I cannot imagine she takes rejection very well.'

'She probably has. She was chatting to Mr Charles and they have gone out for lunch. She started talking to him, and from the moment he answered she moved her stool right up to his and ignored me completely. Looks like I am nothing to her now!'

That's how women feel a lot of the time with fickle men.

'Sounds like a lucky escape for you!' That's what we tell each other afterwards. 'Peter, have you met the maintenance guy?'

'Oh yes, Bill, he's great.'

How can everyone else know he is Bill and I don't remember him? Why?

'He used to be a manager at some construction company. He'd worked his way up from being a teenager helping out on sites, but an accident at work saw him sacked. After that nobody else would touch him, especially at his age. We are really lucky to get him, he really knows his stuff. He works very efficiently and I think he appreciates getting the job. Older people can be like that.'

I knew Peter wouldn't be able to resist adding a bit of gossip. But what he said is different from Maria's take on Bill, and my experience of him. Maybe it's a guy thing, but that's unlikely.

'I've got to go, it's getting busy around the bar. I don't want any fights over who is next!'

Peter is so professional. He's in his last year at university, and only doing the job to make money during the holidays. He is yet another person who has something bigger to do in the future. Everyone seems to move on to greater things, they have careers. I have a job, and stay here. Staff turnover is very high, but I am Sally, the permanent fixture at reception. The managers are never around, they claim to be busy doing so-called 'interviewing' or 'recruiting' or 'in personnel meetings'. Looking at CVs seems to take up most of their day. Sometimes new staff get dumped on me for a day so they can 'experience' reception. They are a pain – people come to check in and they think they are being ignored, muttering about why it takes two people to work one computer.

Staff working with me ask dumb questions, I guess they want to sound interested even if they are bored sick. 'Why are you doing that?' I want to tell them to just shut up and stand there. Usually by the afternoon they think they know how to do the job. I mean, as if it were that simple. They pester me to let them have a go at checking someone in. It's a nightmare – a little information is dangerous. They start to press buttons, then pester me as they don't know what's happening. The guests get annoyed it's taking so long to check in. I often have to redo the whole thing, and that really pisses the guests off, and makes me look bad. Yes, mirror. It's good old Sally. You and I will probably still be here twenty years from now!

*

Oh no. Here comes Mrs White with sonny boy fitness. I bet they are looking for Mr Temple to complain that I implied the fat kid is fat. What's she got rolled up in her hand?

'Look what I found in the room!'

Don't you dare slap magazines on my desk! Who do you think you are?

'A magazine?'

'A pornographic magazine!'

'Oh, where in the room was it?'

'Under my son's bed!'

'How did it get there?'

'I assume it was left behind by the previous occupant, we don't have disgusting stuff like that in our house!'

'Housekeeping surely would have noticed it.'

In fact, some in housekeeping would never miss a porno mag!

'Well, they didn't! It was right under the middle of his bed!'

Hmm. Sounds like sonny boy has been caught out. I bet it's his. He's looking at the floor. Yes, you brat. Blame housekeeping when it's you. I imagine you lie all the time, especially at school, and blame other kids for everything.

That's why you have no friends. I'll get you, you wait and see.

'Your son's bed is a temporary bed. It was put out just before you arrived in the room. It would be pretty well impossible for housekeeping not to notice a magazine on the floor, especially with that cover!'

'Are you accusing my son of lying?'

Yes.

'No, I am saying that it's a bit of a mystery.'

'He brought it straight to me when I saw him with it in the room! He was as shocked as I am. Weren't you, son?'

'I was shocked.'

Look at me when you say that. You can't. Liar. Tossing off is probably your favourite exercise. I wonder how many calories your fitness tracker calculates for that? She should let you keep the magazine. Good exercise.

'Well, I can only apologise. I'll have a word with housekeeping.'

'We better get a discount too!'

Off they go. What a happy family. Some people are weird, I'll never understand how they can live with themselves. They are so miserable about everything, and don't seem to be able to enjoy anything. Worse, they take it out on other people, especially people in jobs where you cannot answer back. One day...

*

'Flowers, you know why I live alone. Should I accept that or try to make compromises?'

Living alone is not always the sign of an 'independent' or strong person, as some people may think. Sometimes I feel imprisoned by my mind restricting me, as if it's trying to pen me into a limited sphere of life. With my job, meeting people all the time and my polite behaviour towards them, people think I am such a nice person that I must be outgoing and confident. Nothing could be further from the truth. I spend most of my life scared. I have to deal with everything. Nobody else is there to help me. I find my work mentally exhausting, having to say one thing and think another.

By the time I get home I just need to crash. I live from day to day on the edge of my nerves. My only escape is my night-time travel in front of the TV. What about a partner and sex? Do I miss sex? I'm not sure. The sacrifices I would have to make to sleep with a man I did not feel comfortable with are not worth it. I simply would not enjoy it. I do think about sex, and see attractive men all day. I look forward to going to bed and playing with my vibrating egg, which works perfectly for me. I find porn films boring, and do not understand why people watch them. Having said that, based on the number of people who watch them at the hotel, they seem very popular!

*

Aha! Here come, albeit slowly, my jolly seniors' outing! These are real seniors, over seventy, not the TV advert so-called seniors 'over fifty'. How can you be a senior if you have not even retired? When I am fifty, no way will anyone call me senior, although people can feel free to offer me the best bus seats! Maybe not, I'd probably blush with embarrassment. If it's a kid I'll think, how cute, then two seconds later think, you're making me feel old, you bugger!

'Good afternoon, sir, welcome to the hotel. I understand you are all off to a show tonight. How nice!'

'They make me come on this trip every six months. I'd be much happier at home without all this fuss.'

I hate being told what to do. That's one reason I left home, and why I've stayed single.

'Which show are you going to see?'

'Haven't a clue.'

'What's it about?'

'Haven't a clue!'

'I bet you are looking forward to it though?'

Time for my cheesy grin, good enough to be in any stage performance!

'No, I don't care. It's probably some stupid musical! The women who organise the trip like watching dancing and singing along with the tunes. My dancing days are over, so why would I want to watch young men leaping around singing?'

I would! The women will be exited, but I suspect most of the men I check in will go through the same conversation with me, even if, in the end, they secretly enjoy it.

'Here is your room key.'

What's that guest doing behind him, prodding him? What does she want?

'Don't forget your drinks vouchers. You get a free beer or wine, you know.'

OK, OK. I was just getting around to that.

'That's right, here are your vouchers.'

What does she want again?

'They try do you out of the vouchers. Make sure you get them all.'

'I don't want vouchers. I don't drink alcohol, the doctor says it's bad for me.'

'You take them, you can always give them to me.'

Ah. Now I know what she is up to! I bet she gets quite a few extra glasses of wine from other people's vouchers!

'Do take your vouchers, you can use them for soft drinks too!'

Got you, lady!

*

'Don't you have group check-in elsewhere? I've been here for ages behind these pensioners!'

What? Oh. Oooh. Scary American guy.

'I am sorry. Good afternoon, how can I help you?'

'Akkad. I have a room for two nights. It's booked under the name Smithson.'

I have a real-life Prohibition gangster in front of me! Slick hair, slimy personality and gangster suit. It must be the fashion in New York. The guy would be comical if not for his stare: icy cold, that of a murderer with more than one kill to his name.

'Yes, here we are. You requested the top floor, right?'

'The suite.'

'Yes, it's a pleasure to have you stay with us, Mr Akkad.'

I wish I had a camera, nobody will believe me. Oh, the shoes! Just look at those shoes!

'Is something the matter?'

'Oh no.'

'Get on with it then! I haven't time to waste. How fast is the Internet here?'

'I am told it's high-speed broadband Wi-Fi, but the speed depends on how many people are using it. It is complimentary.' It's free, so don't whinge. I am tired of people complaining about the Internet speed. 'There is your key. Oh, by the way, two people were asking for you earlier.'

'What? Who?'

Eeek! That expression is the kind of smile that chills to the bone.

'Oh, err, they would not leave their names.'

'What did they look like?'

'A man and a woman. The man was in a suit, looked like an office worker. The woman looked a bit old-fashioned.'

'What did they want?'

He is so weird, looks like he could kill me. It's not my fault they came and asked for you. I'm just trying to be helpful, you ungrateful, scary shit.

'They wouldn't leave a message. They just asked if you were staying here. I said that nobody under that name has a reservation, and anyway, I would not be able to say – client confidentiality.'

Now the couple behind him in line are starting to fidget, the husband looking at his watch, craning his neck around the blockage in front of them. They'll soon be pulling faces, and then start muttering.

'If they call again let me know, but don't tell them I am

here. I'm not expecting anyone, and nobody is supposed to know I am here!'

'OK, I'll try and make sure the other staff know.'

'Why do you have that notice on your desk? It's a service agent's job to deal with any situation. You shouldn't need to hide behind meaningless threats from management!'

'I have been told to leave it there. I don't like it.'

If he doesn't like someone he could probably kill them with that devil smile. That would be his type of abuse.

Phew, he's gone, that's a relief. That smile is pure evil. Now, Mr Stretchy Neck.

'Good afternoon, how can I help you?'

'About bloody time too!'

That was a nice reply. Somehow I expected it.

*

Mrs Smith and Pooipoos are back. The poor pooch must be exhausted after all that exercise in the handbag! She's coming over here, and smiling. Why do I get so nervous when some people smile? What's up?

'Hello, Sally!'

Say something complimentary, Sally. If it is bad news that might help soften it.

'I do like your outfit.'

'Yes, I bought it especially for this trip. I like bright colours. But look, Pooipoos has your bow!'

The dog has the same bow as I have! What on earth does that mean?

'How cute!'

Not. Should I be insulted or flattered? I can't imagine it's the latter!

'Pooie liked your bow and now he has one too! Can I photograph the two of you together? Maybe you can hold him?'

Is she suggesting I look like a dog? Why did she do this? Maybe it's vengeance for putting her next to the lift shaft? If I do this she can go around the hotel, showing people I look like her dog. I can imagine her holding up the excuse of a dog and saying to the staff, 'Who does this remind you of?' I'm sure she could be such a bitch.

'I really cannot touch the dog, health and safety. Remember the mints.'

And I don't want dog hairs on my uniform!

'Aw, that's a shame, the bow looks very sweet on you, and Pooie!'

'Thank you.'

Don't kiss the dog, it's gross enough as it is having to look at it. I think she paid me a compliment, and she is still standing here. Something tells me she may actually want a photo of me, and not so much the dog. Hmm.

'I see you have the notice. Do you get a lot of abuse in your line of work? I should imagine you do, that's why you need the sign.'

'Not really. It's the hotel manager who wants the notice put there. I prefer not to have it, but he insists.'

'Men can be very domineering. I find it's best to just let them think they are the boss and ignore them when they are not around. Fortunately my husband takes many business trips, so I get plenty of breaks from him!'

Is she actually trying to be funny?

'I am sure you miss him.'

'Terribly, but we like our space to do our own things. Don't we, Pooipoos?'

Why is she so chatty? Maybe she's lonely.

'I like being alone, I enjoy it, but it's hard work having to deal with everything myself.'

'Oh no, you need a man to support you. Let them deal with everything, they like the control. Can I tell you a secret?'

Why do people always ask you if they can tell you a secret? It's like the burden of knowing something may be too much for you to bear!

'If you want to.'

'This bag is fake.'

Shock-horror face required, Sally!

'Oh my!'

Phew, I just managed to avoid the 'I thought so' expression.

'Yes, I'm obliged to use it as he bought me it. He thinks I think it's authentic. But when he's away I don't use it, except for taking Pooie around. He has occasional accidents, so I wouldn't use an original designer bag for him!'

Poor Pooiepoos! I don't know what to say.

'Anyway, I've got to go, he needs his lunch, don't you?'

Well, well, well.

'Flowers, what do we make of all that?'

Maybe she is embarrassed about the bag, and saw I looked at it suspiciously when she checked in. She probably wanted me to know she knew it was fake. That she wasn't dim enough not to realise. But why the ribbon on the dog? I am not sure about that.

*

'Good afternoon, how can I help you?'

'I have a room for one night – the name is Mr Anderson, but I think the reservation will be under my company name as they are paying for it. Here's my business card.'

No. It's under your name. I feel a whinge coming on.

'Let me see. No, the reservation is in your name, and not paid for. But that's fine. Do you have a card I can charge the room to?'

Here comes the whinge, I can see his face stiffening up.

'But my company said they were paying for the room.'

'I'm afraid they don't have an account with us, so you will have to claim it back when you return to work.'

'But that'll use up all my credit.'

Your credit? Surely it's a company credit card.

'I'm afraid there is nothing I can do about that, unless you wish to pay cash for the room?'

'No, no. How will my personal, non-work-related expenses appear on the bill?'

Aha! The standard porn movie watcher's question.

'Any bar or restaurant charges appear as *bar* or *restaurant*. No details.'

'And any other things?'

Definitely a porno guy! Do I tease him? Yes, I am in pink pantie girlie mode now – if only he knew!

'Room service appears as *room service*.' That's not what

he wanted to know. 'The Internet is complimentary.'

He's struggling here. He wants to ask, but cannot. I'd better put him out of his misery!

'Oh, and movies in the room just appear as *room movie*. No details.'

Is he relieved, or was that an orgasm?

'Thank you.'

For what? He's on business expenses. Anything he has to pay extra for, he's going to moan about. Anything paid for by the company will not be good enough. All this makes him a good Whinger of the Day candidate. If the company had an account with us then I would have to take care of him, but as I've never heard of his employer he's going into the whinger room 1308. I might as well, he'll complain anyway. Maybe, when he comes to check out, if I mention the movie he'll be so embarrassed he might not even complain!

*

'Good afternoon, Santa! What's on your sleigh on this afternoon delivery round?'

'You'd make a cute elf!'

You haven't seen my holiday season outfit. Only my stuffed toy pets get to see that.

'I'm the wrong size!'

'You look just right to me!'

How tacky.

'Groan, that's terrible, even by your low standards.'

'I came to you as I have no time to wait for them in the office – they look busy.'

'That's a poor excuse.'

'Anyway, this is for one of your guests, a Mr Akkad.'

'Who?'

'Mr Akkad.'

What do I say now? He's not supposed to be here. I could do without all this man-of-mystery crap. But I don't want to upset him.

'I have nobody of that name on the reservations list. But leave it. Maybe someone will turn up for it.'

'I've got to rush! I'm on a hot date tonight. It could have been you!'

'In your dreams!'

In your wet dreams, more like. I wonder what she's like. I imagine she is probably a nice young girl who thinks he is wonderful and has dreams of marriage and babies. Did I want all that fairy-tale stuff once upon a time? Maybe I would have considered it if the chance had come along. It just never happened.

'Mr Akkad, it's Sally at reception. A package has arrived for you.'

'But nobody knows I am here!'

Somebody obviously does.

'I'll ask the concierge to bring it up.'

'OK.'

How can nobody know you are here when you have people looking for you and a parcel mailed to you?! Gosh, he's odd.

'Alex, it's Sally at reception. I have a package for Mr Akkad in the top-floor suite. Can you take it up to him?'

'I'm busy.'

'You are always busy. It'll be worth your while. You have to see this guy. He's a strange one, dresses like a gangster. He's straight out of a black-and-white movie!'

'Maybe it's a gun, drugs or Prohibition alcohol!'

That's my boy, buy into the story. Talk yourself into wanting to do this. It's no longer Sally telling you to do it.

'I can't imagine the guy drinking at all. He's so uptight! Oh, and he has said that if anyone asks for him, he is not staying here.'

*

Well, well, here comes the boat guy. It's nearly 2pm, so that was a good lunch.

'Good afternoon, Mr Shedfield, how can I help you?'

'Sally, sweetheart, are you definitely on for a drink after work?'

'It looks like you've already had one, Mr Shedfield.'

'Please call me John. I only had a light lunch, I'm saving myself for you!'

'I'm sure. Can I ask you something?'

'Fire away!'

I don't want to sound stupid, but he was useful on the notice.

'You said earlier that nobody calls you the GRM at work.'

'That's right. Why do you ask?'

'Well, our hotel manager, Mr Temple, has started calling people by their job title initials.'

'Don't you have names?'

'That's exactly my point – we even wear name badges. He's been on some management training course and now we are all letters, not names!'

'Oh, he misunderstood the course. You use letters when discussing organisation structures, not for the staff names! If there were two receptionists on the desk during the same shift they would be GSA1 and GSA2. The rostered duty manager is the RDM. So if GSA1 called in sick, what could the RDM do about it? But in reality you would ask, "What would Frank do if Sally called in ill?"'

'So, how do I get him to stop doing it?'

'He will eventually. You should try taking the piss, or repeatedly not understanding what he is on about.'

'He seems oblivious to all that.'

'Keep at it. Make sure the others don't encourage him. They may be having a laugh but that will only make it worse if he doesn't realise!'

'The younger staff use the same expressions. I thought they were all having one big joke. But no, it seems they learn this stuff at hospitality training college.'

'Ask them if they are taking the piss. I hope they are!'

'Thank you so much for your help.'

'See you later. You owe me one!'

No I don't. Damn, damn. I was just beginning to feel like we were communicating. You saying something stupid like that right at the end ruined everything.

'Flowers, why do people keep saying I owe them one?'

Don't people do anything these days without expecting something in return? And men – why do they so often say something idiotic at the end of conversations? It's like the excitement of sensing they are getting close to catching their prey goes to their heads! Nevertheless, that was nice, my first sensible conversation with someone in a while. He explained things really clearly, even if he can be a jerk. I feel I could talk to him, possibly about more than just work matters. Well, maybe.

*

'Alex! I see you survived the encounter with the man who is not here.'

'He only opened the door wide enough for me to pass the package through. Not even a tip! You owe me one for that.'

No I don't. I fully expect you to get a tip for taking something up to a room, or delivering room service. Don't waste my time pretending you haven't received one. We poor receptionists hardly ever see tips, and we are the ones who take all the flak from the guests!

'Did you get to see him?'

'No, he stuck his hand out and asked for it, then shut the door. Not even a thank-you. Maybe he was naked!'

*

Now who's calling me? Oh, what a surprise, it's Mr Anderson, my potential Whinger of the Day.

'Good afternoon, Mr Anderson, it's Sally at reception, how can I help you?'

'The TV remote does not work.'

Now that will ruin your porn film plans!

'Oh dear, is it a problem with the TV or the remote control?'

'The remote – oh, and also the light on the small mirror in the bathroom doesn't work either.'

'I'll ask housekeeping to check them immediately.'

I'd better call Maria, I'm not sure how long he'll wait before calling me back, saying, 'You told me you would' etc. Especially if he's hanging on for a film!

'Maria, room 1308, the TV remote and vanity mirror light aren't working. Can you check it out?'

'The whinger room? Ha-ha! I know what it will be. It's a cursed room, haunted!'

'Just go check.'

'It'll be the batteries. Ghosts always steal the batteries from the remotes and mirrors. It's as if they're considered complimentary, like the toiletries in the bath room. Do you know some spirits take the light bulbs too? As a result, management sometimes accuse us in housekeeping of petty theft. Terrible things, these ghosts!'

'It's not ghosts.'

'Well, guests never own up to doing it, so it must be ghosts!'

*

In come Lily and her mum from the zoo. They are chatting away, and Lily looks very excited. They obviously had a good time and now have lots to talk about. They clearly don't need a partner or brother or sister to have fun. Lily has a big stuffed snake. I don't have a snake in my collection of animals at home. I wonder what meal I would have to cook if I did have a snake?

*

Flashy light time!

'I'm coming, I'm coming.'

Maybe we should see if they make a flashing phone that does different colours depending on the extension. Yes, then we could ignore the red flashing from Mr You Must Keep The Notice On Your Desk Temple! And no flash for Mr Akkad as he's not here, the invisible flash! Seasonal or holiday colours would be nice. Green for St Patrick's, bunny pink and chick yellow for Easter. Green and red for winter holidays.

'Good afternoon, Sally at reception speaking, how can I help you?'

'Hello, this is Mr Lane in room 1703.'

Oh, it's the only one in the group of pensioners who wanted a high floor. No worries about using the fire escape for him!

'And how can I help you, Mr Lane?'

'Well, I've found a pair of shoes in the wardrobe. I assume they've been left by the previous guests.'

'I am sorry, I'll get housekeeping to come immediately and remove them.'

'Well, actually, I rather like them and wondered if I might keep them? They are my size.'

What? He wants to keep them? What do I say? Tell him the guy's dead, so yeah, why not? What if the dead guy's wife wants them? She'd probably think someone took them when she was busy at the hospital. Maybe she left them deliberately. Perhaps she never liked them but he insisted on wearing them, probably just to get at her!

'I'll have to check if the previous occupants still want them. I'll have housekeeping bring them to lost property for now.'

'Do you mind if I keep them on for now? They look really good on me.'

Oh no, he's wearing them!

'Mr Lane, I think that you had better wait until we know.'

Time for Maria to feel as hassled by me as I do by her.

'Maria, it's Sally. The guy in 1703 wants to keep a pair of shoes he found in the wardrobe.'

'What? They'll be from the dead guy!'

'Well, I cannot tell him that, can you bring them to lost property?'

'I'm not touching them! Evil spirits!'

I guess that's why housekeeping left them in the room: evil spirits! Probably the same ones that take batteries and light bulbs!

'Please, get someone to bring them down and take them to lost property.'

*

Why is nervous Mr Hill standing around in the middle of the lobby? He's been there for nearly thirty minutes now. He keeps moving a little towards the main door, then back. He looks over at me, but when I catch his eye he turns away. I wonder if he's trying to pluck up the courage to come and ask me something. He looks a bit comical really, pulled by invisible forces in different directions, swinging between the two. I'd better say something.

'Mr Hill, can I help you?'

'Err, no, thank you. Well, do you have a message for me?'

'Let me see. No, nothing. Are you waiting for someone?'

Now, that would be a surprise.

'Err, well, yes actually. Oh, here she is now.'

What? Who? A woman? Where? Off he goes, with that toddling walk, to the lobby doors.

'Have a nice time!'

Damn, I cannot see anyone from this angle. A woman. Well, that's one for the books. I am sure I've never seen him with anyone else here before. Oh, he's coming back in. Bloody hell! She can't be much over eighteen. Look at that girl strutting her stuff. No wonder he's nervous. Naughty Mr Hill. I guess I never really knew him. Over all these years I never discovered if he's married, has children or is a pervert. Now I really want to know!

*

Ah, the tired family seem to have recovered from their long journey. Looks like they are off out for a late lunch. They look rested, all clean, fresh clothes, tidy hair. Like a little line of ducks really! How sweet.

'Flowers, do I want that?'

It's so difficult to know what you really want. There are pros and cons to everything. How does anyone decide, yes, that's what I want? My life feels shrouded in question marks. I'm never able to see clearly because of them. They block any new route or change in my life. Sometimes I wish I could blow them away. But then, would I like that?

*

Oh! Mr Shedfield, I mean John, has changed his shirt and trousers. Wait – did I just think of him as John, not as Mr Shedfield? I wonder why? Hmm. He looks a little smarter, more formal than he did at lunchtime. He's making an effort for someone. I wonder if that's for me.

'Sally! You are off at three, aren't you?'

Who's done his homework? Following our little chat after lunch I am more confident about seeing him. But I must stay in control. I told him no, and even if I wanted to change my mind, I cannot. It's just too weak.

'Yes.'

Let him lead this, then the slap-down.

'So, how about just a little drink?'

What? Now I am reduced to 'just a little drink'! What happened to a night out? Maybe he overspent at lunchtime, or more likely he has a date later.

'I told you I have other plans tonight, and don't forget company policy.'

'Stuff all that. Come on, you look like you could do with a good time!'

Not the type you are, or at least were, thinking of, matey.

'I am sorry. Now, is there anything else I can do for you? I have other guests to attend to.'

'Well, you have my phone number if you change your mind!'

I won't.

'Goodbye, Mr Shedfield!'

'John!'

'Flowers, for all his cheesiness, he is attractive.'

He dresses nicely, has groomed hair and a cute arse. But he does need to stop forcing that smile. It probably comes from having to deal with guests on a cruise ship all day. I'm a bit surprised my smile isn't that bad by now! Mirror, what do you think? Is my face sagging with old age? Is my cheesy smile drooping? Hmm.

*

Hurry up, Katie, my shift is over. Why do some people arrive for work exactly on the hour, within a second of their starting time? Why not get here a few minutes early so I don't have to stay a few minutes extra? It's mean. *Tip-tap, tip-tap* – hurrah! I would recognise that tapping of heels anywhere. How the hell she can stand all evening in those shoes I have no idea. I've warned her, it'll come back to haunt her one day!

'Hi, Katie! Helen is not here yet. I am sure supervisors are always late as they are paid a salary, not by the hour! Just a thing about Mr Akkad in the top-floor suite: he's not here. That is, if anyone asks, he is not staying at the hotel.'

'What?'

'Yes, I know, it's daft, but a little mysterious. He looks like an old-fashioned gangster, so you won't miss him! And he has a shit-scary smile, and a look that could kill!'

'Wow. Can't wait!'

'Oh, and Katie, you'll never believe this! Mr Hill's here with a young woman. I reckon she's only just eighteen! They went to the bar and then up to his room! They are still up there.'

'Really? He's the nervous guy, right? Sweats and blushes when he talks to you?'

What, you too? I thought it was just me who caused that reaction. Even though I am not interested in him, I feel disappointed.

'That's the one. You should have seen what the girl was, or rather wasn't, wearing. The whole bar turned around to stare when he walked in with her. He might be nervous, but he's obviously not shy in other ways!'

CHAPTER 6

TIME TO GO HOME!

'Well, flowers, I made it through the day!'

I'm sure people are getting stranger. The longer I stay in this job, the more bizarre the guests seem to become. The dodgy couple looking for weird Mr Akkad. Then there was that Brandon. I'm still not sure where I have seen him before, it cannot only be at the mall bar. Mr Charles has probably been eaten alive by Miss Wilks. It's a shame I never saw at least one of them return – it must be a good long lunch.

Then there is Lily. She reminds me of myself when I was younger. She's made me think about my past. I'm feeling sensitive about things I haven't thought about for years. What do I say about John? It may have been nice to see him, but I need to get my head together. He would be too intense and pressuring, overexcited at the possibility of getting into my panties. It's been an emotionally trying day. I need to clear my mind and get to know what I am really feeling.

'Flowers, let me whisper to you.'

We don't want the notice to hear. I'll try to think of something I can do to get it removed whilst I'm at home tonight.

'Goodnight, flowers!'

Tonight I have homework. I fix everything myself, a true tomboy. I am so proud of the skills I have had to learn. I can now fix everything! In the past some things in the flat were falling apart, not just because of money, but because I couldn't work out how to fix them. This was really upsetting, as I like everything just right, working as it should be. I couldn't really afford tradespeople, and I don't want strangers in my home. Also, they may not approve of how I live, and the place isn't perfect. I had a life, especially when I was young, of people not approving of me, or complaining about the slightest imperfection. I couldn't handle the sense of rejection I would feel. If something breaks I need to try to work out how to fix it. Now, after several years, I am a bit of an expert with my overalls and toolbox!

Today's 'homework' is to fix a dripping tap. Plumbing is more complicated than you think. Things are different sizes, and you must have the correct tools. I have to pick up a washer on the way home. I am now an expert at changing tap washers! I used to let the taps drip, but the sound stopped me sleeping. I studied how to do it. The nice old man at the DIY store gave me the tools and told me where the water stop tap was. So it's all OK!

As usual, tonight I want to travel, that's my escape. Since our guests come from all over the world, I would like to visit those places too. Alas, I cannot afford it – my rent is too much for that. So, after the giraffe and I had a nice safari in Africa yesterday, tonight I am going to Italy! Italy is a problem. Which stuffed animal should come join me on the sofa? I have no particular animal associated with Italy, so I guess my good old standby the cat will be with me tonight.

You see cats in Italian films, so we will feel like we are there! She'll enjoy seeing the other cats and discuss with me all things Italian, especially the weather, clothes, architecture and history. It will be like having a friend from Italy showing me around! The safari was nice, but salad is not very filling, so it's pasta and a pizza tonight, with a bottle of Chianti. There are nicer Italian wines, and one day I will treat myself, but this is all I can afford this week, and I like the straw-covered bottles. I guess one advantage to having a partner is that you can have the finer things in life, and the cat could could have sat between us, watching TV. Ah well. I am not sure whether to watch one of those old black-and-white romantic films based in Rome. As today has been stressful with the notice, and inspired by the strange Mr Akkad, maybe it's a good idea to watch a gangster film. I'll get some ideas from the Mafia on how to deal with the notice!

Now, a quick check in the mirror. Yes, Sally is presentable enough for the commute home. It's 3pm and I'm out of here. I must remember to change my nails and phone cover to pink for tomorrow. I'm a girl after all! Shop, take off make-up, drink, read a magazine, eat in front of the TV, bed, egg in nest, try to sleep. I'm sure I'll be fine.

TUESDAY

CHAPTER 7

GOOD MORNING!

I feel quite excited today. It's a pink-and-red stripy bow day: girlie on the outside, flirtatious inside! I felt miserable by the time I left work yesterday, so let's hope today will be better! Let's check the mirror. Good: you cannot see my suspenders through my skirt. Pink nail polish, lipstick and phone cover, and I know I have red panties on. The cruise ship doesn't leave until tomorrow, so maybe John will get to see me after work!

*

Oh my! Lily is up at 7am again and chatting to the flowers! Why do they get up so early? She's obviously telling the flowers about her zoo trip yesterday, she keeps showing them the stuffed snake. How sweet!

'Good morning, Lily!'

Oh, just a little smile for me and then she runs off. Obviously whatever it was she was telling the flowers is a secret between them. She's run off into the breakfast room, so presumably her mum is already in there. I wonder why Lily is no longer talking to me – just a flash of a smile and she runs away. She was so chatty on the first day when she saw me talking to the flowers. Maybe she thinks that they are my flowers, and somehow she is stealing my friends when she talks to them? She is very young to start feeling guilty about things, isn't she? Oh, her mum has just come out of the toilets! Why, like yesterday, does she need to go for another pee, having just left the room? I really don't get this.

'Well, flowers, it looks like you have a new friend!'

Maybe she is imitating me. But why? I can only guess what secrets she was telling you. I know you won't tell. She probably likes having friends to talk to. Having a single parent could be boring for a child. Her mum can only have so much energy and time for the girl.

'But flowers, don't get too attached!'

People only stay here for a short time, then disappear, usually never to be seen again. I hope I don't smell of too much garlic after my lovely trip with the cat to Italy last night. There were not many cats in the gangster film. Next time it will be a romance, there are always cats in Italian romance films!

'It's a pink-and-red stripy ribbon day!'

Yes, I needed the change so I can feel right for talking to John – Mr Shedfield.

*

Why is Matt grinning?

'Good morning, Matt, how was last night?'

'Nothing to report, although Katie says our usual hooker

went to the fourth floor. Craig was manager last night and he reckons she went to your charmer boat guy's room!'

He would, he'd love to get into my panties and would say anything to put me off any potential rival.

'I think Mr Shedfield thinks he has no need to pay for sex.'

Why do I feel the urge to roll my eyes at this time?!

'But I reckon it's the strange guy, the one that looks like a '50s gangster! Katie said he called down to complain the Wi-Fi was too slow, and the hooker turned up thirty minutes later. Guess he decided to go for the real thing if he couldn't get fast enough action on his laptop!'

Matt thinks he is so funny, but I know better.

'No, he's on the top floor, and remember he's not supposed to be here anyway, so surely he wouldn't call a hooker!'

Oh no, here comes Alex. I guess he can see we are chatting excitedly, so probably feels he is missing out on something.

'What's the fuss about?'

'Hooker game!'

'It's that businessman, Mr Charles, has to be!'

You are so predictable, Alex. Anyway, he's in Miss Wilks's clutches. Mind you, he did ask for the fourth floor.

'So, Sally, your bet?'

'I think that hooker goes all ways, so could be the woman in 1405, Mrs Smith. She was a bit too nice to me yesterday afternoon – she dressed her dog in a bow like mine!'

Ha-ha, the thought of that got Alex all excited!

101

'They should have asked me to come join them! I'd show them what it was all about!'

Alex, you are such a jerk, and I bet you couldn't – I doubt you are very imaginative at all!

'I think the point is that she didn't want a man involved! She's married to a guy, but that means nothing. Shoo now, guests are coming from the lifts.'

I hate staff hanging around my desk, it spoils the look of it. They make the space around me look all cluttered, a mess. One thing I am not is messy. In any case, they talk crap most of the time so I am not that interested in what they have to say anyway! Oh my, what a coincidence, here comes Mrs Not A Designer Handbag Smith.

'Mrs Smith, good morning, how can I help you?'

'Hello, Sally. I left the room service breakfast card hanging on the door last night and it wasn't picked up!'

Why didn't she just call down, rather than coming to see me?

'I am sorry, shall I order it now for you?'

Oh, well, well. Our hooker is coming out of the lift. It's as if Mrs Smith was trying to distract me, no surprise there.

'No, I'll pick something up myself and take it up.'

Now, let's have a look at this card – yep, two breakfasts! I'm sure one was not for the dog, the order's for continental breakfasts. If it had been the full breakfast maybe it could nibble a sausage, I don't think it's capable of chomping on anything! Mind you, she is not allowed the dog in the restaurant so she would have to have room service. So Mrs Smith does swing both ways. I wonder if she comes and stays in a hotel to have her other needs met when her husband is away? Maybe she is actually in a bad relationship with him, but can't get out. She doesn't seem to work, so maybe that's the trap. I can't imagine not working. It's difficult enough finding someone else to share your life with, but to be married and trying to form a meaningful same-sex relationship on the side must be hell. I guess she has to make do with the odd stolen, or rather paid for, moment.

*

'Flowers, I have a plan to get rid of the notice!'

I was too busy to tell you earlier, but we'll kill it! If I knocked it off the desk Mr Temple would suspect me. So, we must work together to get a guest to 'accidentally' knock it off! If we leave it behind the mints, and I make it stand a little too vertical, the slightest nudge from the bowl of mints will cause it to topple over onto the floor and smash to pieces! People move my mint bowl about all the time, which really annoys me when they don't put it back where it goes. They'll be upset they broke the notice, but they shouldn't have moved my bowl! Clever Sally, eh?! This is so exciting!

Let's see what's in the overnight book. Oh, that would have been annoying – a room alarm clock went off at 3am and wouldn't stop. I can just imagine the embarrassed panic, trying to stop it from disturbing everyone in the rooms around! I'd better call Maria.

'Maria, it's Sally. Did you hear that someone's alarm clock went off at 3am and they couldn't stop it?'

'You can't blame housekeeping for people not setting the

103

alarm correctly. If they can't work the things they should ask reception for a wake-up call!'

'It seems that they didn't set it, it just went off on its own. Housekeeping are supposed to make sure the clocks don't have an alarm preset when doing the rooms. Apparently they could not stop it. They unplugged it from the wall, but it kept going!'

'It must have had a live battery in it! They are lucky, the batteries are usually flat in the clocks. As they are a backup to the mains nobody notices if they are dead, or have been stolen. Anyone can see the stop button on the clock, though, so why didn't they press that?'

'One of the night guys took it away, and removed the batteries. Can you check a new clock has been put in the room? I'll have to deal with them when they check out!'

Maintenance, concierge, restaurant, bar, housekeeping. Yes, good old Sally has to take all the shit from customers for them, and not a tip to be seen.

*

Mirror, you have to say my pink-and-red stripy bow looks particularly good today! Oh, it's Mr Shedfield coming out of the lift. Please don't come over here, I'm not quite ready for you. I need to get my head around all this. He can see I'm looking in his general direction. Oh, no. Breathe in and try to relax.

'Good morning, Sally!'

'Good morning, Mr Shedfield, how can I help you?'

'You look very serious, Sally.'

And? Actually, I am making a real effort here to appear formal, and normal.

'I take my work seriously.'

'You should smile more. You have a pretty smile, but it's hidden most of the time!'

Creep. I smile at everyone. But I wonder if I have given away a different, secret smile.

'You mean one like this?' Fake, silly smile time. Shit, did I really just do that to a guest? 'I'm sorry, I shouldn't have.'

'That was funny. You are quite the comedian, aren't you?'

What? Where does that come from? No I am not. I am not funny at all. If this is a chat-up line it's going wrong for him.

'I have never been able to tell jokes.'

'I bet you can, but you don't need to tell a joke to be funny. Just observe life around you, humour is everywhere.'

I don't get this. Where is this leading? Is he getting at me?

'Nobody ever laughed at my jokes – they didn't get them, and in fact people were not sure if I was serious or not. Even worse, they'd think I was serious, and therefore weird. They'd say things like, "That's not nice", "Don't be stupid" or "You think you are funny, not!" I tried telling jokes as a kid, but nobody laughed and so I stopped.'

What did I say? It just came out. No, this is really private stuff. A guest is not allowed to know it. Why did I tell him? I feel naked. Please start talking to me, I need the time to calm down.

'In our line of work, Sally, dealing with the general public, you have to be very careful what you say.'

105

I suppress everything, a consequence of my childhood. My opinions didn't count and resulted in punishment or abuse, so I stopped saying what I thought. Since becoming a teenager I have kept everything to myself. Even today, I only express opinions to the flowers and mirror at work and stuffed animals at home. It's safer that way.

'Yes, I know.'

'I am bad at telling jokes like the long ones people tell in comedy clubs. I can never remember the lines correctly anyway. In fact, I often wonder afterwards what I was laughing at – was the story really that funny? But you can be very humorous in normal conversation. All you have to do is put two things together that you don't normally associate with each other and it's generally funny! Unfortunately, the world has become too politically correct and some people take offence when you do that, so choose your audience wisely!'

Interview over. This is far too personal for me.

'Did you want anything?' No, Sally, hold it, calm down. That's not the standard question to ask, you are getting rude. He's got to you, just chill, girl. 'I mean, can I help you with anything?'

'You're wearing a new bow and nail varnish, I see! See you later, time for breakfast!'

A wink! He actually winked at me! Who does he think he is? People will think he did get me into bed, or very close to it, last night! How embarrassing. At least he's gone straight off to breakfast. He has no idea what the bow represents. At least he noticed the change. That's nice. But I suspect he prefers red nail polish – he's probably that type. I am red underneath, though. And him, well, from behind, he does have a nice body. Takes care of it.

'What do you think, flowers?'

He shouldn't have winked at me. It's as if there is something special going on between us. It's for me to decide if there is or not, not him.

'Flowers, look at my nails.'

What do you think? I'm not happy with this shade of pink, it doesn't match the phone cover. That's not just irritating, it looks bad, cheap and quite embarrassing. These suspenders are scratching me, so I'll replace them with hold-ups. I'll have to pick some up at lunchtime and, of course, I'll need to change to a pink-and-red spotty bow! But why was he talking to me about jokes? Is he having a joke with all this chatting up? Why was I so sensitive about my not telling jokes? I never tell guests anything personal about myself. You must never reveal a thing. There is a barrier that separates you and the guest and keeps the relationship professional. You must never, ever cross it. Disaster lurks on the other side.

*

'Did you have anything from the minibar, madam?'

'Well, you know minibars! I only ever have sparkling water and whisky. I don't like whisky, but it's the safest thing in the minibar, you know!'

'Really, why is that?'

'It's the previous guests – in fact it could be anyone from weeks before!'

'Err, why? What makes you say that?'

'You know what people are like! They drink the miniature vodkas and gins, then refill the little bottles with tap water and screw the lids back on really tight so you cannot tell! They even do it with the still water! Mind you, at your prices for bottled water who can blame them?'

I know. Housekeeping are always getting told off for not checking the bottle seals. I can't tell her that. I'm not getting drawn into a debate on prices with this one.

*

Lily and her mum are heading to the lifts after breakfast. Well, look – her mum has gone to the loo again. Here comes Lily, with eyes only for the flowers!

'Good morning, Lily!'

She is ignoring me and whispering to the flowers. I wonder what she is saying. I cannot hear, and don't want to upset her by appearing to listen in. Maybe if I bend down to look like I am getting something out of the desk drawers she will let down her guard a bit.

'… and I had toast and marmalade. Mummy had scrambled egg. She has gone to brush her teeth – her new boyfriend Steel is coming to pick us up shortly, so she wants to look good.'

Ah, but why not brush her teeth in the room? Steel is a great name for a guy, instantly gives you an image of someone you would want to meet! If I had a boy maybe I'd call him Steel. I'll have to stand up, my knees are killing me. Her mum is out of the toilets, tapping away on her phone. I wonder if she goes to the loo to make calls she doesn't want Lily to overhear. I know people do that when they're having affairs. Some people are in the loos several times during a meal! They are on holiday and I guess it must be hard to find time to be private if you have a child with you 24/7.

'Hi, Lily, did you enjoy the zoo?'

'Yes, thank you.'

A quick smile and she's running off back to Mummy.

*

Here comes old Mr Wood. I don't know what's up with him. As I didn't get to check him in last night I'm not sure why he's here alone, he's usually with his wife. He's also dressed quite racy for him, even got sneakers on rather than his usual brown shiny shoes! It's amazing what you can do to rejuvenate a pensioner!

'Hi, Sally, time to check out!'

'That's early for you! Mrs Wood not around?'

'Oh no. She died.'

Oops, foot-in-mouth time!

'Oh dear, I am so sorry.'

I'd like to ask more about her death, as women usually outlive their men. But maybe I've pushed my luck too far in this conversation already.

'Don't be, you weren't to know, and she had a good innings. I am up here in town sorting out the legal stuff. Now I have got to leave early to get back to feed the dog and cats!'

'It must be hard for you, coping with everything alone.'

'Oh, it is, Sally. But a fine young man like myself shouldn't take too long to find another woman. Here's my card, I had one hundred printed but doubt I'll need them all. Look, there's my mobile number if you fancy a date! I'm also online now! You see, I even have an email address, hot stuff, eh!'

I'm not sure about that.

'You seem very well organised.'

You seem in way too much of a hurry to move on. I'm sure she was here only a month ago.

'No point feeling sorry for myself. Learnt that in the military!'

Indeed. I guess you are now on a mission to get a new cleaner and cook of a wife ASAP.

'Anyway, got to dash, don't want the animals getting stressed! Don't forget to call, I'll be back to go out on the town soon!'

'Bye!'

*

I wish I could be that organised in my private life. Or do I?

'Flowers, what do you think?'

If you lose someone in your life then that is bound to leave a hole. But what do you do? You can either try to fill it with another person, or change the way you live and fill it that way. But I don't have a hole in my life. If someone came into it I would have to make a space for them. At least I am under no pressure to make a decision quickly. Mr Wood could take his time finding a replacement. He's in a rush now, with all the chores he suddenly has to deal

110

with. But if he gives himself a bit of time he may find that he will naturally fill the void. In a short time he may even start wondering if he really wants to patch up the space with someone else. They won't be exactly the same, and may turn out, over the longer term, to be a liability.

'What about me, flowers?'

Should I take up his offer? He's a much older man. He's got a solid pension, obviously a good one as he can afford to stay here regularly. Why not take up his offer? When he dies I'll be set for life. What? Did I just think that? Agggh!

CHAPTER 8

HOW WAS YOUR STAY?

Here comes John, out from breakfast. Oh, he's not coming my way. He's not even looking this way. Ah, he's chatting to Mr Hill's young woman from last night by the look of it. They are going up in the lift together. You hussy.

'Flowers, why am I so annoyed?'

Why is this bothering me? I've done nothing other than reject him, or be cold. OK, the bow says something, and he noticed it, but he doesn't know the real meaning. I was just getting to know him a little and he does this to me! Mirror, look at me. I look so old. I certainly feel it. It's not worth competing directly with rivals over a potential partner. If the person really likes you they will give you the time and space you need. Even if, whilst waiting for you, they do get involved with someone else, they should be discreet about it, be sensitive to how you feel. Not chat you up and then behave like a shit because you won't be rushed into something you are not ready for!

*

Smelly Mr Green is emerging from the lift. It's only one bloody floor and you are in your twenties. He probably has the same attitude to getting washed, lazy toad. I can feel myself gagging just looking at him! I hope he has had a shower. I'll have to deal with him whilst other guests are using the lift before I can spray air freshener in it. Emergencies like this are too urgent to wait for housekeeping to turn up. After using a smelly lift the guest will come see me next and complain. Yet again, Sally gets to deal with the flak as if it was my fault!

'Good morning, Mr Green, how can I help you?'

Hurry up and reply, I don't want a line of gassed guests forming behind you!

'I'd like to check out.'

And what's the little word that makes Sally helpful? No, he's not going to say it. No please from him. At least he's not smelly, hurrah! He may have cleaned himself up, but the thought of that smell will linger in my mind. I could never, ever be attracted to him. Men, like women, should be expected to smell nice all the time.

*

Oh, goody, Mr Charles is calling. I wonder how yesterday went. It's from his room, not Miss Wilks's – I thought she would have him in her lair by now. Tee-hee!

'Good morning, Mr Charles, it's Sally at reception, how can I help you?'

'I need to send a fax, any chance you could help?'

At this time of the morning? I thought you would be having breakfast in bed with Miss Wilks!

113

'If you take it to the business centre they can do it for you.'

You know this, you are a regular guest. What do you really want?

'But it's a bit private, I wouldn't want anyone I don't know seeing it.'

I don't know you!

'They will let you fax it yourself if you wish.'

I'm not doing it, I am not your bloody secretary!

'I wondered if you could pick it up and send it for me?'

No way! And I am not coming to your room. I guess Miss Wilks is not there. She knows you better than me by now so get her to do it. Maybe she caned you and you are too sore to move! Mind you, after parading her through the lobby in front of me yesterday, she could well be in his room to be shown off again. Jerk.

'I'm afraid I am not allowed to leave the desk unattended, and my supervisor is nowhere to be found.'

For once a missing Frank is a good thing!

'OK, I'll have to bring it down. I've got to be on my way to my presentation.'

Your presentation? No, it's the company meeting, you are just a small part of it. The fact you are not there already suggests you are not that important. I'm still wondering why he would ask for a room on the fourth floor. It's completely out of character, he's always a top-floor guy. Miss Wilks is on the fourth floor. I wonder if they already knew one another.

*

Here comes Lily with her snake in her arms and her mum to check out. It's been nice seeing her around. Reminds me of myself, well, when I was young and naive. At least her mother seems to want her, which is more than can be said about mine.

'Good morning! How can I help you?'

'We're checking out.'

'That's fine. Lily here has been chatting to my flowers.'

'Yes, she said you talk to them, that's made quite an impression on her!'

'I see you two get up quite early.'

'I have a job so we are used to getting up early so I can leave Lily with a childminder before work. It's become a habit, even on holidays!'

'How did you manage when she was a baby?'

'Lily's dad was not interested in family life, but fortunately I had my parents and sisters living nearby to support me so I was able to return to work after a short time. They still babysit a lot for me.'

'Well, it was lovely seeing Lily. I hope to see you both again soon!'

I mean that.

'Flowers, what do you make of it all?'

My family would be no use, especially if I had a girl. I think I would need a partner if I was to have a baby. You don't have to have one, but in my case I would need one as there is nobody else, only poor old me, and I don't have the money for a childminder or nanny.

*

115

Aha! There goes Miss Wilks to breakfast, alone. Maybe Mr Charles is as organised in bed as he is at work and her time allocation is up! She's completely ignoring Peter the barman again. It looks likes she definitely has her catch in Mr Charles. I wonder if she knows he's married. Maybe she doesn't care. He certainly doesn't.

'Look, flowers.'

Only a few seconds later and there goes Mr Charles. What a coincidence, I am sure! He's in his suit, fax in one hand and attaché case in the other, smartly into breakfast. You should never go to breakfast in a suit as it picks up the smells. You may be able to keep your food from spilling, but there are always others to accidentally collide with you. Like people who drink red wine on airplanes. If the plane suddenly moves you're covered in red. I think you should only drink white wine or preferably champagne on flights. Not that I'll find out any time soon. Why take your case into breakfast? You are in a suit, so people can tell you are a businessman. You don't need a case to hammer the point home.

Oh, he's back quickly. Maybe he just said a quick hello to Miss Wilks and is now off to the business centre and then, I guess, to 'his presentation'.

*

Wow, he looks fit! That's a very nice expensive-looking suit, worn just loose enough for comfort, but muscles clearly bulging! I wonder what he does for a living – weightlifting businessman? If he was a sporty guy he should have a jacket and trousers. The only sporty people on TV who wear suits are the commentators – oh, and the team management. Maybe he's a sports manager, he looks old enough to be.

'Good morning, how can I help you?'

'I have a room booked for the day.'

And? I am not a mind reader! Who are you, or do you expect me to recognise you?

'What name is the booking under?'

That's my emergency reply for any case where I am expected to recognise someone. In order to save embarrassment for the celebrity, you have to make it seem like their agent, assistant or even sponsor may have made the booking.

'I am trying to keep this secret, nobody is supposed to know I am here. Lean closer and I'll whisper. Wicklane, Brad Wicklane. I am here for an interview with the city's football club, but it's all hush-hush. We don't want to risk any of my fans seeing me here, do we? That would cause a scene!'

Gosh, he's full of himself. Yes, I have heard of him. He's past his use-by date. People only interview him out of politeness. He was great once, but now he's just deluded. And stop looking down my shirt at my chest. Yes, I have lovely firm boobs but you are going nowhere near them, so get your face away before you start to drool!

'Oh, it is you, Mr Wicklane. I thought I recognised you.'

Naughty Sally, you should not tell lies! So why, if you are being so discreet, are you standing here in the lobby in front of me? If you are so famous don't you have 'people' to deal with things like this?

'They say I'd be a great addition to the team, but I'm not sure I want to move, as great a city as this is. I have my fans back home and wouldn't want to desert them.'

For someone avoiding publicity he's managing to hang around the lobby long enough. I bet he is craving to be noticed by someone!

'I have a great room for you on the top floor, it's a double aspect. You should be safe from your fans up there!'

'Actually I'm a bit funny about heights, can I be on a lower floor?'

Ha! So much for the sports star, more like a chicken with muscles. Cluck-cluck. More like an old rooster!

'There you are, Mr Wicklane, room 1305, the lifts are across the lobby.'

'You can call me BW.'

BS, more like!

'OK, BW.'

Jerk. Jerk chicken.

*

Here comes Peter. I feel a shot of Italy coming on!

'Hi, Sally, your morning espresso macchiato!'

'What is "morning" in Italian?'

'*Mattina, questo è la sua espresso macchiato di mattina!*'

Oooh, I could fall in love with that.

'Say it again slowly.'

'*Questo è la sua espresso macchiato di mattina.*'

118

Oh, yes, yes, yes.

'Thank you.'

'Did you see who you were just talking to?'

'Yes, a man.'

He is supposed to be here incognito. No way am I gossiping with you, Peter.

'Don't you know him?'

'Should I?'

'Yes, it's Brad Wicklane, the sports star! Do you think I can get his autograph, or maybe a photograph with him?'

Well, I guess that since he's been recognised I cannot be blamed for talking about him.

'Keep it quiet, he doesn't want a fuss about his presence. Why would you want his autograph or photo with him? You're not a kid!'

Mind you, you would have been when he was at his peak of fame.

'He was a hero of mine!'

He's a jerk.

'Did you see that boat guy go up with the young girl? They were sat at separate tables, but he got up as soon as she did and they went upstairs together! Wasn't she with an old man yesterday? Hookers are getting younger by the day!'

Yes, I saw them, but did not know that! Bloody men. You shit, John. Sally, smile as if you don't care about a thing in the world.

'So it seems.'

'See you later!'

'When they stay in the hotel, Australians say, "See you later." It doesn't mean they will see you again any time soon!'

Peter is one of the biggest gossips in the hotel, he sees everything from the bar and shares it. It's not good to gossip so much, even if it does help pass the time and give some relief in the quiet moments. I am discreet, I think or see things, but would never tell him. For someone of his intelligence it's almost demeaning. I won't feed his gossip, or risk him going to others and saying, 'Sally said…' One day his gossiping will get him into trouble. He, like most gossips, often gets the wrong end of the stick. He makes me worry over things, and I sometimes get stressed by his visits. It's nice to get the gossip, but I regularly feel worse, not better after seeing him!

*

'Flowers, now there's a surprise!'

The couple who were searching for Mr Akkad yesterday are coming out of breakfast. I guess they met up with him. I didn't see them arrive, they probably turned up before I started. Oh, they are coming over here.

'Good morning, you found your Mr Akkad then?'

'Why, is he here now? We hoped he may be around at breakfast, but he wasn't.'

Shit. How do I get out of this?

'No, I thought maybe you had found him and gone to breakfast with him.'

That did not sound convincing. I am feeling a sense of panic. Earth, please open and swallow me up, I could be in trouble here. Can they see it in my face? Force a big smile. Anything other than looking scared.

'We sent him a package yesterday, and it was delivered. You signed for it.'

Oh no. That was sneaky of them. How do I get out of this?

'I sign for packages all the time, but have no idea if they are collected by guests. They are kept in the office.' Come on, Sally, quick now, think of something. 'If nobody picks up their deliveries they are returned to the courier.' Wow, that was impressive. Who's a clever Sally?! 'Would you like to leave your names, or a contact number, so if he does come I can tell him?'

'No, no.'

Off they go, looking a bit confused, but at least they are leaving. I half expect that Brandon guy to turn up now, but there's no sign of him. It's probably too early in the morning for someone who spends a lot of time in bars! I'd better tell Mr Akkad. He'll hate me for saying it, but at least he'll know. Hopefully no killing the messenger today.

'Good morning, Mr Akkad, it's Sally at reception. I thought you might want to know that the two people who were looking for you yesterday were in the hotel again this morning asking for you.'

'What did they say?'

'They had breakfast in the restaurant, they had hoped to see you there. Apparently they sent you a package. They still refuse to leave their names or a number for you.'

He doesn't sound that upset. Strange, yesterday he was really angry.

'I said you hadn't checked in, and there was still no reservation in your name.'

'Good, nobody must know I am here.'

'Of course, Mr Akkad.'

Now I am panicking because he is so calm! I hate it when people change personality completely. How the hell am I supposed to know how to interact with them?

*

Mrs Smith just went from the lift to talk to Alex. I wonder what about? Now she's off back to her room. She has totally ignored me. Good boy, Alex, come here and tell me. This is his slow, cocky walk – he knows something I don't and he's trying to tease me by taking his time. Idiot.

'Your hooker game girl has asked me to book a car to take her to and from the airport.'

'And?'

'And that's it.'

'You didn't find out why?'

'Why should I?'

'You felt the need to tell me this gem of information, but it's half a story! You should have followed it up with something. Receptionists are great at doing that. I would have asked if she was meeting someone from a flight, offering to organise the driver to have a board with their name on at arrivals.'

'She might be going to pick up another woman, I didn't like to probe.'

You are useless, Alex. You hit on me, but badly. You haven't a clue about women, or probably men for that matter!

'Try again when she leaves!'

*

Ah, Officer Hackness, right on time.

'Ten o'clock and all is calm.'

'Yes, Sally, it is. But we don't pound a beat any more.'

'Did you ever have to do that?'

Damn, I should never have asked, he'll chat forever now.

'It's part of training. You have to get to know your area. I believe we cannot just sit behind computer screens or in cars and solve everything that way. Real life is not like they sometimes show on TV programmes. I am not old-fashioned, technology has its place, but talking to people is the best way to prevent crime. Technology is better for investigating afterwards, if you ask me!'

So, you don't come here just to get discounts on tickets from the concierge, chat to pretty me, and have a coffee because you like the way we make it? You are actually saving the world when you come here?

'I thought the idea was that technology helps prevent crime before it happens. Isn't that a better thing than dealing with it afterwards?'

'Solving crime is my job. You can waste lots of resources on trying to prevent crimes that may never happen. With budget cutbacks I sometimes think those upstairs have got some of their priorities wrong.'

'I spend all day in front of a screen, that works for me!'

'Very funny, Sally. Well, I'd better go to get my coffee.'

I didn't think that was funny. I do spend all day in front of a screen, and it works for me. Maybe I still don't get humour.

123

Here we go. It's Mr Anderson – did I spot my Whinger of the Day?

'Good morning, Mr Anderson, how can I help you?'

'I'm checking out. I should have been up much earlier but the noise around the hotel was too much, I hardly slept. I need my sleep, you know! It's not helped by the air conditioning, it's so noisy, and blows straight onto me! Doesn't anyone else complain about these things?'

Yes, they do, and the hotel does nothing about it. It's too expensive to fix, Mr Temple always says. We have budgets to live by, I am told. As if I don't know! You try living on my wage!

Some whingers try to bait me. They say things like, 'Don't you think the concierge is a bit rude?' Even if Alex is, I try ignore what they say. It's often better not to get drawn into their conversations. To ask, 'How was your day?' and just ignore what's said in reply works for some hotel receptionists. I don't like that. So I don't ask that question. I am supposed to do so, but I only ask it if I really want to listen to the reply. At least Frank is never around to pull me up on it!

'Here's your bill.'

Do I mention his movie? He did watch the porn. I wonder if he enjoyed it. The porn films we have here do tend to lack much of a storyline. He probably had an orgasm in a couple of minutes and switched the TV back over to the sport!

'Is it possible to have it split into two bills so my personal expenses don't appear?'

Come on, it only says, *room movie*. OK, I'm sure your accounts department will giggle, reckoning you watched porn. Someone may even come and ask what film you watched to try to embarrass you. You shouldn't watch a film in your room if you cannot take the heat! I can split the bill, so I guess that will be a big relief for him. Can I tease him on this? Think I can, I have pink in my bow after all!

'I am not sure the system will allow that.'

Yes it will, but it's a pain to do it.

'Please try.'

'Let me see.' I am doing you a favour here, so don't even think of annoying me afterwards. 'OK, that's done.'

'Thank you.'

'Well, flowers! That was disappointing!'

Mr Anderson turned out to be a low-level whinger. No prize for me today.

*

Here we go again, Mr Temple is approaching, and no Frank within a mile!

'Where's the MOD?'

'What?'

'MOD.'

'Do you mean Frank?'

'Yes, Frank.'

So why the hell didn't he just say that? MOD, manager on duty – Frank's more of a manager off duty!

*

125

'Good morning, Mr Hill, how can I help you?'

Who's the nervous one now, Sally? I'm not sure where to look. I wonder if he knows the girl was also with John?

'Err, I am ready to check out.'

Oh, she's over by the bar, with a coffee. I didn't notice if she came out of the lift with him.

'Did you have a nice stay? Was the room OK? You mentioned yesterday you weren't sure about it?'

'Err, did I? Oh, well, yes thank you.'

Oooh. Here comes the girl! This will be interesting. I want to know why she was with John, I can't wait to ask. But maybe that would upset Mr Hill, who always seems minutes from having a heart attack.

'Hurry up, Daddy! I need dropping off before you go to your meeting!'

Daddy? Sugar daddy?

'Oh, he's your father?'

'Yes! My dear old dad!'

Do I believe her? Who cares, I have to play along anyway. If it's true then mentioning John is not too bad a thing to do, is it?

'I saw you come out of breakfast this morning. Did Mr Hill not want any breakfast?'

Why am I asking her rather than him?

'Daddy never comes down for breakfast. He likes to have room service in bed and watch the TV! I love the buffet, there's a much better selection of things to eat, and I can go back a few times!'

Now, say this as normally and nonchalantly as possible.

'Didn't I see you leave with Mr Shedfield?'

'Oh, was that his name? It was purely coincidental – we both left our tables at the same time.'

Get ready for a big blush and stare at the floor from you, Mr Hill!

'Well, Mr Hill, you have a beautiful daughter!'

'Why, thank you!'

Yes, he's blushing.

'One day you'll have to introduce me to Mrs Hill.'

'Mummy? Oh, there is no Mrs Hill. They got divorced years ago. In fact Daddy really likes you, but he's too shy to ask you out on a date!'

What? Oh no, a cringe moment. The poor bugger. I'd better try to be nice.

'Mr Hill, you never said anything.'

'He doesn't! He gets really shy in front of women he finds attractive. I wish he'd get a girlfriend, he needs a woman to organise him!'

If your mum was anything like you he probably never got a chance to talk.

'Well, thank you for suggesting I am attractive. But I'm sorry to disappoint you, I'm already taken.'

It's only fair to lie to him, poor sod. Next time he'll be more relaxed in my company without feeling under pressure to chat me up. Mirror, do I look attractive? Maybe to Mr Hill I do, but what about everyone else?

What do you think, flowers? Am I attractive? I feel relief that she wasn't actually with John. I still think she could be a hooker, playing along for Mr Hill's benefit. There is plenty of acting needed in prostitution! But why did John get up to leave at same time she did? Was it deliberate so he could try to chat her up? Maybe he was watching her.

*

Oh no, my phone cover really does not match my new nail varnish! It's a very different pink. I must go shop at lunchtime for a new shade. John noticed the change of varnish, but I can't risk him noticing that it doesn't match the phone if I see him later. He can't tell now as my mobile must be kept in my handbag – personal phones are not allowed on the desk.

Ed the courier looks tired after last night. Maybe he was lucky with whoever she was! The unlucky girl.

'Good morning, Santa looks a bit sleepy!'

'Great night, last night!'

He really doesn't get it. It must be immaturity, or maybe he's just dim. No way am I going to want to sleep with him when he's bragging about what he got up to with someone else. He is no catch, no prize, he's just an idiot.

'Don't you have an excuse today as to why you have to come to my desk rather than going to the office? I guess you just want to tell me all about last night.'

Silly Sally, don't encourage him!

'Oh no, they were all on their phones. I've got three packages that need signing for and I've no time to hang around.'

They probably all pick up their phones and pretend to chat as soon as you walk in the room! Maybe they didn't want to know how your evening went either. Strange, you don't seem to be particularly forthcoming about your date.

'So, how did it go?'

Not that I am really interested.

'It was really great! Got to go!'

Well, that was bizarre. I can only guess it was a disaster. He was probably up all night, frustrated and playing with himself and computer games! Or was he lucky? Maybe it went too far – that girl may really want a baby and now he is shitting himself. I could see him on a reality programme having some argument in front of a couple of rather unattractive, sad young girls over who he's screwed and who's the father of the baby!

*

Why are you walking over here with a menu? This is reception, the restaurant is behind you. I don't just check people in and out. When there are no guests at the desk I have lots of admin to deal with that you don't see. You are about to interrupt me, break my concentration, and I'll have to start what I am doing all over again. I have to deal with reservation issues, picking up calls from others who are never around or too damn lazy to answer. They are probably too busy on their mobiles.

'I'm looking at the restaurant menu. Is any of this suitable for nut, berry and seed dieting?'

What? Are you serious? Can't you tell what a nut, berry or seed is? In any case, you should know, you are the one on the diet! I assume you actually read a dieting book, and didn't just look at the cover and want to sound 'cool'.

'I have no idea, there are so many diets these days you lose count of what's allowed in what.'

I am taking the piss – can't you see?

'It's how we used to get food before supermarkets appeared.'

'Really? How interesting!'

I am *not* interested, can't you tell I have better things to do?

'Oh, I need to know. Will this be gluten-free?'

Oh, come on! How the hell am I supposed to know?

'Try to ask the chef. Or if you ask Peter the barman over there, he'll find out for you.'

My turn to have a cheesy smile, totally gluten-free, and enough saturated fat to kill you!

'OK, thank you. One can never be too careful, can one?'

Don't tempt me to reply.

*

John is in the lobby. I wonder why? I am relieved about the girl, but still suspicious of his real motivation towards her. I hate feeling jealous, really hate it. Next I'll start worrying and it will eat away at me. Especially if I wake in the middle of the night, my imagination will run riot. I'll feel miserable, and there will be nothing I can do about it. It's much better to avoid relationships altogether.

'Hi, Sally, you look a little stressed.'

It's not over you, if that's what you are implying, idiot.

'It all comes with the job! What can I do for you?'

Please say a drink after work. Did I just think that? Oh no!

'No, nothing, I'm bringing my bags down to leave with the concierge. I don't want to have to carry them around when I check out. By the way, if you ever need anyone to talk to, I am all ears.'

And all hands too, probably. Come to Johnny, let me make you feel better. Bollocks.

'Oh, I did mess up a little thing earlier, and I'm not sure if there will be consequences.' It's really annoying having to wait for a response. Your imagination gets the better of you. 'But it's probably nothing.'

'Worrying is not good for you! It won't change a thing. Just live and learn!'

'Easier said than done.'

'So what was it? I will always have a minute for you.'

Puke. What rubbish.

'A guy is staying at the hotel and some people want to see him. But he's said not to let anyone know he's here.'

'And you did?'

'Not exactly. But the guy may be upset. He looks like an American gangster, you may have seen him around.'

'No, don't think so, and for someone who's trying to be inconspicuous that's not the best dress sense! I would forget it. Time to drop the bags off, the queue's gone now.'

Forget it? Again, easier said than done. Thanks for not really listening, cutting me off before I finish telling you.

'Have a nice day.'

So, what do you make of that, flowers? Was he just passing time here at the desk, nothing to do with me?

And worse, no invite to a drink. Maybe he'll meet up with Mr Hill's daughter, or his date last night – I assume he had one. Uff. Talking to John helps get things off my chest. He is easy to talk to, even if he is like that with everybody else too. It would be nice to see him later. My break is only thirty minutes so I expect to see him when I get back.

*

Ah, there goes Mrs Smith off out now. I can't tell if the dog's in that fake bag or not! Alex mentioned she needed a taxi to take her to the airport. I wonder why she is going there? Maybe she really is off to meet another woman. She's back to dressing in her frumpy suit – I wonder why she's changed out of her coloured outfit? She isn't looking towards me. It doesn't bother me, she looks focused, but it's surprising she didn't even glance over. Well, she's booked in for another night, so hopefully I'll get to see who it is later.

'Yes, flowers, the world of reception has changed.'

Nobody leaves their keys at reception any more, the little cards are easy to slip in a purse. I used to like the big, clunky keys. That way everyone used to leave them, saying good morning or good afternoon on their way in or out. They would say where they were going or what adventure they'd had. Very polite and nice – the hotel felt more like a family in those days. Looking after the keys made me feel part of the guests' day. Their adventures were mine. There are some guests who come over to tell me they are off out, especially the regulars, and some older guests who miss the chit-chat associated with dropping off keys. Most guests only talk to me when they check in and, with the express check-out box, I often never speak to them again. So, I am left to guess what's happening around me.

'Wow, look, flowers!'

Alex is moving fast! It's like the excitement of his news is obviously too much for him!

'Alex, so, did you find out anything?'

'She's off to pick up her husband.'

No wonder she's not chatty. I wonder if he's back a day early. I hope she's got the hooker's hairs out of the bed, they haven't changed her sheets yet!

'Oh, OK.'

'I wonder if he knows she likes women too?'

Based on that handbag, I wonder if he really cares.

*

Here come the nice family to check out. The kids look excited.

'Go show the kind lady what you have made.'

'I have drawn you a picture!'

'Now, let me see. That's lovely, is that me?'

'I like your bow, so Mummy said I had to draw you from behind so you can see it!'

I wish I was that thin! A view from behind, eh? I wonder how many other people see me as faceless.

'It says, *Sally at Reception*. Very nice. Do I get to keep it?'

'Yes, it's for you. But you have changed your bow! It was red and black yesterday.'

'Today is a pink-and-red stripy bow day!'

'So what is the pink for? I like pink.'

'That's for you to guess.'

What a sweet, puzzled look she has. Her brother looks excited, bursting to say something. Here it comes.

'Your knickers!'

Typical boy. He almost got it, why don't supposedly grown-up men? Time for a cheeky smile.

'No, my nails!'

At least she didn't ask about the red.

'Come on, you lot, we have to go to the airport.'

'Have a safe journey.'

How sweet. It makes putting up with all the shit at work worthwhile. Is this it for the rest of my life? Assuming I could cope with childbirth, and I haven't really thought about that, you never know who will make a good parent. How do I know if I would be any good at it? Can anyone having a child really know if they will be a good parent? It's not just you, it's the partner too, if there is one. How can you know if a partner would be a good parent, even if you think you would be? What if you realise you cannot hack it after the baby's born? That it's not for you after all, and you are stuck with something you really cannot handle for eighteen years or more! What if the kid turns out to be a shit, even if you were a good parent?

I've seen all types of families at the hotel, and you really cannot tell which ones will be happy and which will not based on what they seem to have materially. Life on its own is enough stress without a shit family life added to it. Do I really know what I want, or just think I do? You cannot just

'give it a go' or accept that 'you'll never know until you try'.
It's another life you are talking about. How can anyone take
the risk of having a child?

CHAPTER 9

LUNCHTIME!

'Flowers, it's lunchtime!'

I'm going to change out of these irritating suspenders. I'll pick up some hold-ups at the store, and of course a nice pink-and-red spotty ribbon to go with them. I wonder if John will notice the change in bow. I must dash, see you after lunch!

Today is a salad day! No, not because that woman was on some fancy, fashionable diet! I ate too much pizza and pasta last night with the cat in Italy. Way too many calories. I want to look good for John in case we have a drink after work. It's important I am hungry later, just in case we go to eat afterwards. I am not planning to, but you never know!

There we are, mirror – presentable, but I will look and feel a little different when I return!

*

Oh, mirror, the hold-ups feel nice! They are so comfortable. I can feel the air between my legs. A little swish and the skirt brushes over my bum. Not blushing, am I? I just had time to get a new shade of pink for my nails to match the phone cover. It's better, but now it has dried it is still not right. Just a little tweak of the ribbon, see pink-and-red spots. One sexy babe.

Teeth brushed, make-up restored, no stains on clothing. Good. Here we go, only four hours and I'm out of here, and maybe for the first time in years I won't be alone. Hmm.

CHAPTER 10

GOOD AFTERNOON!

Oh shit, sports star BW has seen me looking in the lobby mirror before I get to the desk. People sometimes think I am staring at them when I'm looking in the mirror. Those guests who like the idea of me looking at them see it as an easy excuse to come to chat. In this case he wants to be looked at. His eyes hunt for the slightest glance to hook on to! Here he comes. Now he's intercepting me, blocking me from the desk. I hate people talking to me on the floor of the lobby, I am only comfortable, and feel normal, when I am behind my desk.

'Mr Wicklane!'

'Not too loud, hush-hush, remember! And it's BW! I'm sneaking off now to my interview, wish me luck!'

Go away, I want to get to my desk.

'Good luck, BW!'

'Your smile is all I need.'

Please go then.

'All the best!'

There he goes, walking slowly across the lobby, a slight turn from side to side with each measured step, making make sure everyone gets a good look at him. No, what? I don't believe it! A guy is going up to him. Ha! He asked if he's Brad Wicklane, and says he thinks he's great! Look at that smile, not just BW, but the guy too! Probably made both their days! Oh no, the guy's coming over here – another obstacle on my way to safety.

'Do you know who that is?'

Let me make this easy for you: I want my desk.

'Mr Wicklane, the football player.'

'Yes, fantastic isn't it?! He's so famous, and I met him! He stopped and spoke to me! Can't wait to tell my friends!'

Please go do it now.

'You should have taken a selfie with him on your phone!'

'Oh yes, why didn't I think of that? I wonder if he'll let me if I go catch him outside. Must dash!'

At last I can get to the desk. Let's hope I've finished my shift before BW returns. He'll be unbearable! Groan, the guy's coming over here again.

'Phew, I was just in time! What a gentleman he is. Look at the photo, great, isn't it?! I can't wait to show everyone!'

'Good for you!'

Now he's showing Peter the barman the photo, he's looking quite envious. I bet he'd love a signed picture from Mr Wicklane behind the bar.

'Now, flowers, do you like my pink and… Who's removed my flowers? Where's the flowers? Who's stolen my flowers?'

Where's Frank? Nowhere to be seen when needed, as usual. I'd better call Mr Temple.

'Mr Temple is out at lunch.'

Typical.

'Someone has stolen my vase of flowers!'

'Oh, yes. They have not been stolen. They had to be removed. A client accidentally knocked the vase over. Frank has taken the bits to throw out.'

'What? My flowers?' I can feel myself shaking. It's hard to concentrate. My leg is twitching. 'What happened?'

'I'm not sure, but it was something to do with the notice on the desk. I think someone knocked it off, and when they reached out to catch it they sent the flowers flying.'

'That notice! I'll kill it, the bastard.'

'I don't think you can blame the notice.'

'Yes, I damn well do.' Shit, I'm starting to cry now. 'I have to go redo my make-up now. I'm leaving the desk. Find Frank and get him to cover until I come back.'

I am shaking, crying and suddenly feel hollow. That vase has been here as long as I have. I feel like I've lost a part of me.

'Stop grinning at me, you stupid notice. I'll get you when I get back, so start shitting yourself!'

*

Mirror, look at me. I've rushed my make-up, it's a mess. I suddenly look and feel so old.

No sign of John yet. I look so rough. He probably won't want to be seen with me looking like this. My eyes are red! Let's see. Oh, he's checked out! Damn him. What a bloody day this is turning out to be, it's going from bad to worse. After the death of the flowers I'm probably not really in the best mood to see him later. On the other hand, I need

140

cheering up. I'll call Alex the concierge – not for cheering up, that could never happen, but to check on John's bags. At least Alex can't see how distressed I am over the flowers. If he saw me like this he'd think it was about John and spread the gossip. I couldn't face Peter coming over to ask how I was feeling, as if he cared. Crap like that I can do without. I am single, live alone and handle my problems my way by myself. I don't need false sympathy. I'm not cold-hearted, I am sympathetic to others. It's just I cannot stand the stress of people making me dwell on things I'd rather forget. I am not weak, pathetic. Not really, I'm just independent.

'Alex, it's Sally at reception. Do you still have Mr Shedfield's bags?'

'Yes, does he want them?'

'No, I just wondered. He checked out when I was at lunch.'

'He wanted to know when your shift ended! Any idea why?'

None of your bloody business! I can imagine him grinning, the shit.

'No idea. Maybe he wants to give me a guest comment card.' That sounded so lame! 'Never mind, thanks.'

Hanging up on Alex is always a pleasure, a release of pressure. I hope John pops back in to see me before he leaves. I need someone to talk to about the flowers. I feel so sad. I've sort of got used to him, and he does listen.

*

141

I enjoy the old theatregoers, they can be really funny and often have had interesting lives. But I have a job to do and they can also be a drain. They come out of the lifts a little confused and mill around the lobby. Today they remind me of one of those films with zombies roaming around shopping malls. What? Did I think that? That's not nice. Where did that come from? Why did I find the thought funny? If I'm getting a sense of humour, is this the right direction for it to take?

'We are checking out.'

Why do so many people think I am psychic? Maybe they are communicating with me via ESP? Let me try. I'll wait a second for the rest of the sentence. Umm, nope, nothing coming by mouth or ESP! Who are you? I recognise many guests but when it's a big group they tend to blur into a mass. I could ask who they are, even 'under what name was the booking', my saviour phrase for checking in people who I am supposed to recognise. If they think I don't know their names, it's a bit of a let-down. For checking out, asking the room number is best. For some reason people expect me to remember their names, not their room numbers, so it works. I do like everyone to feel special, like a guest, not a visitor, nor one of the management's 'clients'.

'Could you remind me which room you are in?'

'Oh, we threw the little key card thing away, but it's room 1401.'

'That's Mr Hall?'

'Yes.'

'So, how did the theatre go last night? Did you enjoy the show?'

'Not really, it was confusing, wasn't it, dear?'

His 'dear' is just nodding.

'Which production did you go see?'

'Haven't a clue, have we, dear?'

Dear is still nodding. She can talk, I saw her chatting in the line with another woman a minute ago.

'What was it about?'

'It was confusing, wasn't it, dear? But there were some animals in it – well, people dressed as animals. You liked the music, didn't you, dear?'

Dear continues to nod. 'Here's your bill, please check it.'

Dear has stopped nodding.

'That's not our bill! We never watched the adult movie channel. Did we, dear?'

Dear nodding again. It's funny how everyone assumes if you watch a pay-per-view movie in a hotel it must be pornographic.

'No? There are other types of film too. Did you watch one of them?'

'Nope.'

'You did say Mr Hall in room 1401?'

'No, we are Mr and Mrs Thompson.'

Groan. Why do people confirm the room number and name, then when they read the bill they decide to be someone else in a different room?

'Let me see.'

Dear has stopped nodding.

'Ah, Mr Thompson, you were in room 1105, an easy mistake.' Three floors of mistake. Never mind. 'Off you go, have a safe journey home.'

If I ever get a partner, please let me keep a mind of my own.

I do not want to be turned into a nodding dog. My parents had one in the back window of our car when I was very young. It was probably there to train me in how to behave!

Ah, now someone I do recognise. Mr Dead Men's Shoes.

'Good morning, Mr Lane. Did you enjoy the show?'

'Boring, they always are. I only come to these things for a change of scenery.'

'And how was your stay with us?'

'Great! The shoes are really comfy, been worn in a bit, you see. There's nothing worse than new shoes for cutting up your feet! Second-hand ones are much better.'

What? Maria was supposed to take them to lost property, where they stay for at least three months. Maybe she really is scared to touch dead men's shoes! I guess there's no real harm done, it's unlikely anyone will come looking for them now.

'Glad you are pleased, hope we see you again soon!'

Walking in dead men's shoes!

*

'Maria, you sound agitated.'

Nothing new in that, but she likes the chance to get things off her chest.

'It's that maintenance guy, Bill! A light fitting has come loose and he's supposed to fix it. How can we do the room with it hanging from the ceiling? It's dangerous!'

'There's nothing I can do about that.'

But that's another health and safety issue – he could have brought the lobby mirror down on his own head, and now he's electrocuting housekeeping! Peter said he had a problem with an accident in the past. But why would Peter claim he was so good at his job? Maybe Bill feels the job is beneath him – he was a manager after all. It could be that he has an issue with taking instructions from women. Maybe he's used to a man's world. That's sad if true.

*

At last, a break. Dealing with that coachload of old folk took my mind off the flowers. Poor things. Why didn't Frank save them? We must have a spare vase around the place. You bastard notice, your time is coming. Hope you are panicking. Nobody will catch you the next time. You'll see.

*

Here come a young couple holding hands. How sweet. You don't see much hand-holding in relationships these days. Such a shame. Shame about the clothes too – are they victims of fashion or do they just have bad taste?

'Good afternoon, well, almost! How can I help you?'

'We have a reservation for one night. The name is Rogers.'

Why are they sniggering? Oh, I get it.

'Yes, here we are. One night, double bed. Do you have any luggage that needs taking up to the room?'

'No, we are fine.'

They are still grinning. Must be the excitement of staying in a hotel. Maybe they feel naughty!

'Here is your key, it's room 1507.'

'Where did you get the background music? It's great, very retro. Reminds me of some old films we have seen.'

Old films? Some of these tunes are from modern classics. You are making me feel old.

'It's the manager's selection. He's older than me.'

Not by much, mind you. How quickly things become old or 'retro' – it only seems a few years ago that these films came out, and yet those kids weren't born then.

'Mirror, do I seem old and out of date?'

It wasn't that long ago I was their age, was it? I know fashions in clothing change, but it's usually just minor changes to styles. Some things never change, like jeans. Well, until that silly thing of having holes ripped in them. Why would anyone want to do that? But hair, that is another thing. I have long hair held up in a ponytail by my bow. I cannot look down at my reservations and have hair in my eyes, can I? So, I have a practical approach. I think hair fashion is much more creative than clothes fashion. But why do young people copy the styles of models? There is nothing worse than someone wearing a hairstyle that does not suit their features! That poor girl, as attractive as she thinks she is, having half her hair shaved off looks plain ugly. And the guy, with just a little long hair on top of his head covered in gel, well, that looks like something a cow would leave in a field, doesn't it?!

*

Mrs Smith has come back with, I assume, Mr Smith. He looks a very smart business or professional man. Not the type to give a fake handbag as a gift. He's coming over here, let's see what this is all about. Why is she staying near the lifts? It's like she is ignoring or even avoiding me.

'The name is Smith – I need a spare room key. My wife only has one.'

I can guess who probably has the other. She's not looking over, maybe she's reading my mind. One thing I am is discreet. I'm not likely to say a thing. Maybe she is worried she might blush.

'Not a problem, Mr Smith, here we are.'

'Thank you.'

He's a very formal type, maybe she had to change out of her bright colours to something that matches him. Or worse, out of clothes she likes into something he likes. She looks stressed. I guess it must be really difficult to change mindsets from having an illicit sexual relationship with a woman and then a few hours later playing the role of dutiful wife. She was so friendly when she came with the dog bow. Now she seems cold and distant again. I feel hurt by that. I thought I might mean a little something to her. On the other hand, I can only assume she has to divorce herself from her feelings for other women when with her husband. She probably has to be cold to avoid interactions that confuse her. That's quite a schizophrenic existence. It surely can't be good for overall mental health.

*

Oh no, here come the Whites. I wonder if they found anything else for sonny boy to play with? Now look at that, Mrs White is staying across the lobby by the cases, away from me.

'Good afternoon, Mr White, checking out?'

Or you have something else to complain about?

'Sorry we are a bit late checking out. Son here was on the laptop and it's so hard to get him off it. I have no idea what kids find so interesting to look at on it.'

Probably porn, now you have taken his magazine away.

'Thank you, Mr White, that's not a problem.'

'It shouldn't be after what poor Son here has been though.'

I'll get poor son yet. Just wait.

'I hope everything else about your stay was fine, Mr White?'

'Yes, no problems. Lovely view from the room.'

'Yes, the higher floors have great views of the town. Did your son have a go at using the stairs to help his fitness tracking?'

'No, he didn't.'

'But I did go to the gym! I ran on the treadmills!'

Walked, most likely!

'So how much weight did you lose over your stay?'

'I burned two thousand calories!'

Isn't that the normal recommended daily calorie intake for a woman?

'But how much weight did you lose? Calories burnt are one thing, but you need to count calories consumed too!'

Big fake smile time!

'What are you implying? My son eats too much?!'

Oh no, here we go again. The parents are as bad as each other!

'To lose weight you need to burn off more calories than you consume, surely?' Calm down, Sally. Don't lose the

148

plot. 'What's the point of counting what you burn, if you consume more?'

Oh hell, he's about to cry!

'Let's go, I can't listen to any more of this rubbish!'

You should have let him keep the porn mag!

*

Someone else is coming over from the restaurant. At least he is not carrying a menu this time. Mind you, the walk looks quite determined, and the face is definitely screwed up in semi-agony! Don't come here to complain about the cooking.

'Do you only have the one bar?'

Impolite sod. Where's the 'good afternoon', or at least a quick hello?

'Yes, although you have a minibar in your room, and we have room service.'

'You should call it a coffee shop, not a bar! The guy in there spends all day making coffees, and I am sick and tired of waiting for a whisky that only takes a few seconds to pour whilst he stands there looking at the machine drip goo into a little cup that takes an age to fill! I guess calling room service to deliver to me in the lobby would be quicker?'

'I'm afraid the room service drinks come from the same bar, so that won't speed things up.'

You have my sympathy, mate, that's why I drink wine at home – no delay in service there!

'You should forget serving Italian-style coffees made by hand. Install a self-service machine in the lobby. They have ones these days that make all the different types.'

149

What, and lose my individually prepared and presented espresso macchiato? It wouldn't even talk to me like Peter does! No way!

'I shouldn't really say this, but there is a nice wine bar just around the corner from the hotel. I sometimes pop in there for a drink before going home – alas, it's too expensive to do that as much as I'd like to!'

Oh shit, it sounds like I'm flirting. No, no, I am not interested at all.

'It looks like the line has shrunk, so better get in quick! Thank you!'

Phew! I hope he doesn't pick up on it!

'This is when I need you, flowers. How I miss you!' The space looks so empty, the desk bare of life, just a leering notice. 'Your days – no, hours – are numbered.'

I don't mean to flirt. I'm not used to dating, so I sometimes forget the innuendos that may come from things I say. Anyone who lives alone gets no feedback from conversations, and so can seem to say the wrong thing. I get lots of conversations here at reception, but it's all structured, and generally polite. I feel bad when I go against hotel policy. This place is like a family, even if it is as dysfunctional as my own. But there are times when I like to help guests. Telling the guy there is a wine bar nearby isn't a crime, is it? The concierge tells people where they can eat and drink. So why do I feel bad when I do it? Surely it's best for the hotel if people use their facilities, even if overpriced? I feel for guests. I understand when they are frustrated or upset. So if I can, I do help. I get great reviews online from guests. I like the feedback, it makes it all worthwhile.

Oh, the young couple I just checked in have come back down. I really thought they would be at it like rabbits all afternoon. Ah, they are off to the bar, but surely not to listen to the 'retro' lobby music. They look embarrassed, almost guilty, talking to the barman. Wine and a beer. They are old enough to drink legally, but with that behaviour I wonder if they are allowed to drink at home. Maybe it's against their religion. Maybe that's why they are here. Maybe they are not allowed to be together at home.

'Flowers, if you were here you would see.'

They have sat side by side, not opposite each other. I never understand why people do that. You see it in the restaurant. Surely you want to face each other when talking. They look slightly uncomfortable. Maybe it's been a while since they last met. Maybe they don't know each other that well after all? But look, now they are touching each other softly. Maybe it was a touch of date nerves. He is so gentle and caring towards her, and hasn't taken his eyes off her from the moment they sat down. He's so attentive to her needs. I wish I could have that kind of attention from a partner. Maybe not. Maybe that would be too suffocating, claustrophobic. But it's nice that he seems to care.

*

Wow. How to make an entrance. All she had to do was walk in through the lobby doors and pause a second. All heads turned. Blue-eyed blonde syndrome affecting the lobby. She

151

is tall, dressed in a smart jacket and skirt, and walks with an elegant swish.

'Good afternoon, how can I help you?'

'I have a reservation for tonight, the name is Elana Karlsen.'

Scandinavian. I should have guessed. She could have been Eastern European, but she has more of a Western European beauty. Oh no, she has brains too, a doctor. Oh double no, she is part of the group going on the cruise with John.

'Dr Karlsen, it's a pleasure to have you stay with us. I see you are part of the group taking the cruise tomorrow. Here is an envelope with information for you from the organisers.'

'Thank you. Why we have to go on a boat for the conference I have no idea. And some people may be bringing children! They are bound to get bored or into trouble.'

She said that with a genuine smile. Not that's it's a bad thing, just bizarre. So often people say things like that and mean it coldly, but this lady, no. I wonder what type of doctor she is?

'I believe there is a storm due off the coast.'

'That's all I need! A boat of panicking medical researchers!'

She is nice, lovely smile.

'I am sure it will all be fine. Here's your room key. Have a nice stay.'

This is when I need the flowers again! I miss having someone to talk to, especially when stressed. Why do I now feel jealous? I have many attractive women come stay in the hotel, and some are also educated and rich. Why does this one annoy me? She is nice, not a bitch at all. So why? Surely not that she is here alone, and will be on the cruise with John? He hasn't a chance with her, not that he won't try. Why am I getting jealous over someone I hardly know? He better not be getting into and messing with my head! No way. But…

Why's Peter rushing over from the bar? It must be important, I'm almost panicking looking at him!

'Hi, Sally, your afternoon espresso macchiato!'

'I'm surprised you didn't spill it! What's the rush? Oh, and what is "afternoon" in Italian?'

'*Pomeriggio. Questo è la sua pomeriggio caffè espresso macchiato!*'

'That sounds a bit of a mouthful, not as nice at the morning version! And the rush?'

'Who's that stunner of a woman?'

Groan.

'I hope you didn't drool in my coffee!'

'She is amazingly attractive. Film star or model?'

'You obviously haven't lived as much as you claim. Anyway, she's too old for you. I can't imagine she'd be interested in you!'

'Miss Wilks was!'

'This woman is class. She's actually a doctor too.'

'I'm at college. We're made for each other.'

'In your dreams.'

'I see the flowers have gone.'

'Yes, it's sad.'

'I saw it happen.'

'You did?'

'Yes. Frank was at reception and some woman put her handbag on the desk. When she went to open her bag the notice was struck, she lifted her arm to grab it and her elbow nudged the flowers and they went flying. The vase shattered, the flowers went skidding all over the lobby. The woman was really annoyed as the dirty water went all over her shoes and splashed her skirt.'

'How did it get in the way of the flowers? I put it behind the mints!'

'I think Frank moved it so that she could get her bag on the desk, it was one of those large ones. Why women need such big bags I have no idea! Man bags are always small, unless full of toys or man magazines.'

What is he on about?

'Toys?'

'Laptop, tablet, tech stuff!'

'And porno mags?'

'No, you know the ones, they have articles for men on having soft skin and looking younger! And pulling girls, and who's hot and—'

'OK, I get it!'

Bloody Frank. Anyone who put anything on the table was supposed to nudge the mints into the notice and knock it flying.

*

What's Miss Wilks doing? I am sure I just saw her put her room key in the express check-out box. She's not due to leave until tomorrow. Why would she leave a day early? Mr

Charles is due to leave tomorrow, so why would she want to go? Maybe I mistook it. Maybe she is like the idiots who put their rubbish in any hole they can find rather than take it to the bin. I can imagine her as an antisocial cow. At least it's Katie who deals with the express check-outs after I leave. But I would love to know if she is leaving early – she hasn't informed me. Maybe she's had enough of him. Maybe the close encounter at the breakfast table was more than she could take. Maybe he told her she was not his type and she is embarrassed and leaving before he returns. Maybe they fought over the cane! Maybe he told her he was married. Oh, so many maybes!

CHAPTER 11

CHECKING IN?

Now that's definitely a single dad! Two teenage girls in tow, both listening to tunes on their phones, totally ignoring him. I bet their mother has sent them on holiday with him and they hate it already!

'Good afternoon, how can I help you?'

'The name is Hobart, I am here with the cruise group.'

With children? Dr Karlsen mentioned something about that. I thought it was a conference or something?

'Let me see, yes, Dr Hobart. A twin double bed room.'

Oh, the kids are listening. I imagine they spend most of the day taking out one earpiece so they can listen and talk.

'I'm not sharing with Sophie! Dad, you promised us separate beds!'

'Sorry, girls, the organisers booked the rooms.'

They seem nice enough, maybe because they are girls, not boys, and he's really nice. Time for that pained expression.

'We do have a rollaway bed but unfortunately I am not allowed to put it in a room with two beds, for safety.'

'No, Dad!'

That came out simultaneously, even with their music on!

'Well, think of it like camping!'

'Our grandad says there is a storm coming, do you think it's safe to go on the ship? Will we get seasick? Bet Kylie will, won't you?'

'No I won't!'

They seem like your average teenagers. Was it the mum or dad that made them like that? Maybe they had a normal family life. I want to ask if they are divorced, but cannot think how to bring it into the conversation.

'I have never been on a cruise, but I understand they are like floating hotels. You will only realise you are at sea if you look over the edge!'

'I'm not going near the edge!'

Earplugs back in now, so guess that's the end of the conversation!

'Here are your keys, the lifts are over there.'

*

'Good afternoon, how can I help you?'

'I have a reservation for one night. Here's the voucher.'

Ah, a holiday trip type. Travel companies often put them in here after a long flight before transferring them up the coast to the resorts.

'Mrs Jackson, so how are you enjoying your holiday?'

'What holiday? I've just arrived.'

OK, calm down, lady. You look way too stressed. I feel a whinger in the making.

'How was your flight?'

'Awful. The person in front put their seat back for the whole journey. I asked the stewardess to get them to put it up, and they did, then when she left they put it back down again.'

I have taken only one flight in my life, from my parents to here. That was exhilarating! I was escaping. I thought going on holiday was like escaping, it's supposed to be exciting. Things like seat positions aren't important. You are having fun. No?

'That's not very nice.'

'It's downright inconsiderate and rude. They shouldn't let people adjust their seats. I wanted to bang on the back of their seat like children do, but you have to put up with the person for the rest of the journey, so I had to suffer!'

Whatever. Oh, shit, and she is not going to stop now. She obviously has a lot on her chest and needs someone to whinge to.

'The food was awful, all in plastic and metal foil. The table was so small everything kept falling off! I was left surrounded by a pile of rubbish and nowhere to put it!'

'Isn't that normal on a flight?'

'This is my first holiday outside of my country.'

Yes, a real Whinger of the Day candidate. You go abroad because it's different. So don't expect it to be like it is at home. You are paying for the experience of something new, not just the same thing as at home with better weather! You are very lucky you can afford to travel abroad, I can't. I can see you will have a miserable time, what a waste.

'That's exciting for you.'

'It seemed like a good idea when I booked it, but I'm already regretting it.'

'Travelling to and from your destination is the worst bit. When you get there you'll be fine!' No you won't. 'Here's your key, room 1308. I hope you enjoy your stay.'

She won't.

*

Ed is looking very tired now, maybe last night is catching up with him.

'Santa's bag heavy today? You look worn out!'

'No, but I'm looking forward to going home. It was so exhausting last night!'

I bet you mean hard work. I suspect you aren't much of a conversationalist.

'Did you spend the night stuffing things down chimney pots?'

Well, I reckon he was stuffing something last night.

'The van's playing up, I've got to get it looked at.'

What's that got to do with anything? Am I supposed to find the state of your van interesting? Is that something you tried to chat with her about last night? Did she look worried, ask what's wrong with it? If she was desperate she would have faked concern. Or is it an excuse to stand around here chatting for a bit?

'So why are you here cluttering up my desk today?'

'Your boss is in the office, so I thought I better not interrupt.'

'Was it anything important?'

159

'Hard to tell. Now, I'm supposed to pick something up from your guest Mr Akkad.'

Oh, him. The mystery guest who nobody knows about. Mind you, he did say he was expecting someone to come collect a package this afternoon.

'Yes, let me call him and see if he has it ready. Mr Akkad? It's Sally at reception. I have a courier here for you waiting for a package you wish to send?'

'Yes, can you send him to my room?'

'He wants you to go to his room.'

'OK.'

He didn't even notice my flowers were missing! If anyone cared they would know how important they were to me. When I was a teenager, would I have gone for him? He has a van, that's useful. He has a job, so his own money. Maybe I would have dated him. I may even have gone on to marry and have kids with him. I hear my mum's voice: Be grateful for what you have, young girl. Girl, girl, girl. Not a boy.

Oh, he's back quick. Why didn't he just go straight out? I guess he'll take any excuse to chat a bit longer to me.

'How was Mr Akkad?'

I wanted to say weirdo.

'Odd, but nice enough to me.'

I'm not gossiping.

'I thought you had a schedule to stick to?'

'Yes, must be on my way!'

Just because someone is not perfect doesn't mean you cannot have a relationship that works. Nobody's perfect, and everybody has a different take on perfection anyway. Maybe when you are young you are more flexible, and both

160

of you can grow together. More likely naivety and hormones cloud the judgement! I cannot imagine growing together with someone now, I'm set in my ways. A relationship would have to be a perfect fit, wouldn't it?

*

Well, a few more cruise ship people have checked in. All Dr This and Professor That. I hope the rest arrive after I leave, otherwise it'll be a busy end to the day. Although they are from all over the world they all speak good English. Strangely, none of them seems to know each other – surely some do, but maybe just not the ones I have checked in. They are all from towns I have never heard off. Nobody is from a major city – well, except Mr Akkad. It makes conversation a bit limited. When people come from a capital city I usually know some of the landmarks and can talk about them, but these all seem to come from the back of beyond. It's very weird – maybe that's why they are here, it's a treat. Well, a week or so on a boat will mean they'll all know each other much better later! Here comes another, he must be, an older man with a bow tie, straight out of an American university I'd guess.

'Good afternoon, how can I help you?'

'Menston's the name.'

I guess that means you want to check in? Or a late check-out? You are supposed to be the intelligent one! Only one Menston on the system, fortunately.

'Ah, Professor Menston. It's a pleasure to have you stay with us. I see you are part of the group taking the cruise tomorrow. Here is an envelope with information for you from the organisers.'

'What? Not more paperwork! It's only a bloody boat, more of a holiday camp if you ask me. Do you know they are letting children come along? It's a damn medical conference! These people are fussing too much. It's as if they are really worried I might get lost and not make it in time.'

'Well, you are a professor, whilst I am sure you are not absent-minded…'

'Who do you think you are saying that?'

Shit, no sense of humour. I thought with the bow tie he must have.

'I'm sorry.'

Eek, now I don't know where to look.

'You and that bloody concierge, are you all insulting in this hotel? He told me I'll have to wait a while for my bags as he was busy. Busy doing what? He was just standing there! When I said I need them now he told me to take them myself. The cheek of it!'

Don't get drawn into this. It's Alex's problem, not mine.

'Oh dear, I am sorry. Here's your room key – oh, and you get a complimentary drinks voucher.'

'A what? Voucher! Not more paper! What's it for?'

'Any soft drink or house wine at the bar between 4 and 6pm.'

'Why 6pm?'

Uff, can't I say anything without getting shouted at? Keep calm, Sally.

'It's quieter at that time, happy hour.'

162

'So I get a free drink when they are half-price? Great! What a deal! No doubt the house wine tastes like vinegar, eh?'

Put it on your chips at dinner, jerk. It's a free drink so be grateful, you shit of a snob.

'It'll be built into the room rate anyway. So I am still paying for it, in fact paying for something that's probably undrinkable and I won't want! I hope they have decent wine and food on the boat, not hotel crap.'

'There are some nice restaurants in the area, close to the hotel.'

'I bet they are all fast food places, and those ghastly food courts where everyone sits around eating out of plastic. I don't want to smell Indian food when I'm eating Chinese! And self-service is, well, degrading.'

I can't say a thing without him pulling it apart. I wonder if he is married. Imagine what that must be like. I think I'd rather not. OK, where's Alex? Oh, ha-ha! He's sneaking over to the service lift, avoiding the professor, I guess. He should learn to do it like our hooker. Eyes forward and a brisk but not too fast walk straight to the lifts!

*

Here comes the boss. Breathe in deeply, after all, you never know when you'll get a chance to breathe out again!

'Where's today's RDM?'

I've had enough of this. RDM? Could be rooms division manager, rostered duty manager, or at this rate a soon-to-be reception desk murderer!

'Which one, the R DM or RD M? The MOD is Frank.'

'I know that, you told me this morning. I mean the RD M.'

What? He understood that crap I just blurted out?

'Probably in the PDR with HR doing his PDR.'

'Shouldn't be, he's due to be with me.'

He doesn't even realise I am taking the piss!

'I'll tell him if I see him.'

This has got to stop, but they are all talking like that these days! Even reception is called front desk, although it's not a desk as I don't get to sit at it, I have to stand all day! And the use of 'front office', well, that's just asking to get 'FO' shouted at you. WTF is the matter with these people?!

*

This guest looks different. Well, I have seen everything, but her combination is odd. Mind you, it does make it more of a challenge guessing what someone might do for a living. Slightly hippy clothing, but very smart bag and laptop case. Could be anything.

'Good afternoon, how can I help?'

'Hello, I have a reservation for tonight, the name's Mrs Kirkstall.'

'Let me see. No, I'm afraid I have no reservation under that name for today.'

'That can't be right, I made it through your reservations centre only a week ago! Here's my email confirmation.'

'Yes, the day is correct but look, it's for next year!'

'What? How could it be? I said to the guy next week!'

How do I answer that? Isn't it your fault for not checking

your confirmation when you received it? Reservations are idiots and you should have booked online? Best to ignore the question.

'Let's see if I can find you a similar room for tonight. Yes, that's fine. Just let me get your key.'

I wonder what she is doing here. I really want to know more about her.

'So, what brings you into town today?'

'I have a meeting with a publisher, I'm writing a book on meals for one.'

What?

'Meals for one?'

'Yes, for people who only cook for themselves.'

Like me.

'That's interesting, do you have any new recipes?'

'Well, you might assume people can't be bothered cooking long meals just for themselves. But if they are on their own then surely they have time to. So I am looking at how to fill up those lonely evenings by cooking complex meals for one! The ingredients are used in small quantities, enough for one, or with a long shelf life. We don't want to be wasteful, and single people are on a tighter budget than couples, aren't they?'

Tell me. A low-paid job almost forces you into living with someone else. But my freedom is worth the financial sacrifice.

'We had a guest today talking about seed and berry dieting – apparently it is fashionable. Do you have that in your book?'

'Oh, good gracious no! This book is about proper meals,

165

starter, main course and dessert! The full three courses, not dieting!'

Is that a triumphant smile? Is she for real?

'Well, that all sounds very interesting. Here's your key and good luck with the publisher.'

Just looking at her is depressing me. If I ever see this book I'll avoid it. On the surface it may sound like a good, practical idea. But on reflection, what it says about lifestyle is depressing. Lonely hours that need filling, portions for one, tight budgets. I won't read the foreword, I'm sure that would make me suicidal!

*

Oh, Officer Hackness! He's coming straight in to me, what's he doing here at this time of day? If it's important the police would contact Mr Temple directly and we would expect them. This is unusual, coming in like that through the hotel entrance, no chat to Alex the concierge. He looks seriously stiff.

'Officer Hackness, what a surprise! How can I help you?'

'Is the manager in?'

What, no 'Hello, Sally'? Two-faced thing. I know he's on business but there's no need to be like that! Imagine a relationship with him. You would have no idea which 'mode' he was in. Mind you, the way he looks it's obviously something important.

'Let me see.'

I can be cold too, so there! No smile, serious Sally time. Stare at phone keypad whilst calling. Oh, here comes Mr Temple straight out of his office, must have seen him arrive at reception on the CCTV. That was quick – he obviously has bugger all else to do other than look at me at the desk all day!

'Hello, Officer, we weren't expecting you, how can I help you? Shall we chat in my office?'

Having serious police business is not good for the image of the hotel. It's OK when they are nice and chatty, but not when on real business with an expression like that! He might scare the younger guests and freak out the dodgy customers! It's good the lobby is not too full, we may have had a few extra-early express check-outs!

*

Mirror, I'm looking tired again. It's already feeling like it's been a long day. I feel really drained today. Maybe Officer Hackness thought I looked bad and uninteresting? He could probably tell and didn't care enough to express concern. I reckon his career comes before his partner, if he has one. If he does, when he is in uniform he probably forgets her, or him.

*

Well, it's Mr Temple again.

'Sally, get me the RDM.'

'I have no idea where he is, Mr Temple.'

There is never a manager when you need one, you should know that!

'In that case you need to come in here.'

'I can't leave the desk unattended.'

'OK, I'll call you at the desk and explain!'

Oooh. I wonder what it's all about! Here we go.

'Mr Temple.'

'Sally, the police are here to talk to Mr Charles. Apparently he may have undertaken something illegal, and we need to deal with this with as little fuss as possible. Do you know if he is in his room? Be careful what you say in front of customers.'

They are my guests, not customers, idiot.

'There's nobody at the desk. Mr Charles? But he's a regular, I can't—'

'I don't care what you think. Is he in his room?'

OK, arsehole. Just trying to help!

'Mr Charles is out at some company meeting. I have no idea when he will be back, he's not due to check out until tomorrow. He spent a lot of time with Miss Wilks, but I saw her leave about an hour ago.'

'Miss Wilks?'

'Yes, she has a reservation for tonight as well. But I'm not sure if she is returning as I thought I saw her drop her key in the express check-out box. I haven't seen her since.'

'Alright. If you see either of them let me know immediately. Do you understand? Immediately!'

'OK.'

Why not ask me to call and find out? Well, this is exciting. I bet that tart got him into this! Idiot. Why do men think with their dicks all the time? You should always be careful doing favours for strangers, or trusting them or taking people at face value. For all the people who chat me up, I never know any of them long enough to let myself get close. Working in this job, seeing what real people can be

168

like, I would never trust in or even believe what I am told. I have seen so many people that lie, cheat, deceive, abuse, con, scam etc. Worst of all is to be set up as a scapegoat. People can be naive. Making someone innocent get punished for something they have not done, or did not realise they were a part of. He did ask for a room on the same floor as her – coincidence or not? In any case, if she has left, maybe she used him, and he gets arrested and she gets away with it. The police weren't interested in Miss Wilks until I mentioned her. Let's hope he's back before the end of my shift.

*

Aw, that's nice, some daughter bringing her old dad and child to the hotel. I wouldn't want to bring my parents out. But that's my choice. He looks smart, and she's well dressed. The child looks well mannered, maybe she will remember the day she visited the hotel with grandad. I don't remember ever going out with my grandparents. They just sat at home and drank tea and talked between themselves. I was told to leave the adults alone, to go play with my doll or teddy bear. Maybe there was something wrong with my childhood. Mind you, people live longer now and are more active than that generation.

'Good afternoon, how can I help you?'

She's letting him deal with everything. She probably wants him to feel proud, not having to lean on the children in his old age.

'The name is Turner, we have a room for two nights.'

'Very nice to see you, Mr Turner.'

Oh, the booking was made by a Mrs Turner. Specifically says Mrs. It's a double bed and a rollaway bed. It's his wife and daughter. Wow, what an age difference.

'I love this place. I used to come here a long time ago with my ex-wife. We loved room 1708, is it possible to have that? I have great memories of it, and it has such a lovely view! You'll love it, sweetheart!'

What? Did he just say that in front of his new wife? She is just smiling. I wonder if she was actually listening to what he said. Maybe she ignores what he says a lot of the time. Perhaps she has to, especially if he keeps referring to his ex. I guess there is nothing wrong with talking about past relationships. It's probably especially helpful if there were issues that still need addressing. But I would hate to think I was a substitute for the last one. Same room indeed!

'Well, we are very busy tonight, but let me look.'

I wonder if the child is his? She is probably about six or seven, but very well behaved. She is standing and waiting, watching the activity in the lobby. Ignoring her parents totally. No clinging, swinging on anyone's arm, or asking questions about everything. She hasn't even asked about the Wi-Fi. I thought all kids wanted that!

'It's your lucky day! I have just to move a few things around and you can have your old room.'

Oh, Mrs Turner heard that.

'Old room, what old room? I thought the hotel had recently been refurbished?'

'Oh, all the rooms have been updated.' Well, it depends if a splash of paint is what you call updating. The bathroom fittings haven't been changed for years. 'Mr Turner specifically asked for room 1708, it has wonderful views. Here are your keys.'

Off they go. The guy's about seventy, about the same as old Mr Wood who was chatting me up this morning. Would it be like that for me and Mr Wood? There are so many issues that come to mind.

*

An hour to go. Come on, John, you'll miss your lucky chance. Why do I feel so bothered? Now I feel like I need to see him. But I'm not needy – I'm Sally, independent of everyone. How on earth did he get into my head?

I really hope the coach of tourists arrive late, I've had enough of today. If the rest of the cruise ship guests and the tourist group arrive at once it'll be too much. Every time we get tourist groups from overseas, reservations mess up. They often get the first and last names the wrong way round. Sometimes it's impossible to match people to their passports. Once a group arrived and the list of guests had been written phonetically, nothing like the actual spelling of the names! I've told them again and again to double-check the lists they are supplied with but they never seem to learn!

*

Ah, here come my longest-serving guests. How nice to see an older retired couple still able to travel independently and really enjoying their time!

'Mr and Mrs Delaney! How lovely to see you!'

'Hello, Sally! Good afternoon to you!'

'So, what brings you into town today?'

'Mary, you tell her, I need to dig out the booking.'

'Don't worry about that, you don't really need it unless you have a common surname, but I know you anyway.'

'Yes, Sally, I think it's ten years now you have been here! It's unusual to still have the same reception staff at a hotel after all that time. I'd have thought you would have moved to somewhere more exotic. You must like it here – I bet you now have some nice man who's keeping you here?'

It's actually fifteen years, and in another thirty I'll have a piss-poor pension to retire in poverty on. Don't remind me how many others have come and gone at reception in the meanwhile. All those youngsters, probably now running hotels all over the world. I am still here. They say the same thing every time: I need a nice man. Well, no, actually, and I don't love it here. I can only just cope with the job. The last thing I need is more stress brought about by change at home.

'Nobody yet!'

'Oh, but you are so pretty. You should be married with children and living together as a nice family by now.'

Thank you, Mrs Delaney, for calling me pretty, but change the damned subject, please.

'So, what brings you into town today?'

'Well…'

'Well' always means, 'This is going be a long one.' Fortunately there is nobody in the queue yet. The Delaneys live in the countryside, and I am sure Mrs Delaney misses having neighbours to chat to, especially women.

172

'As you know, our daughter Jane married a medical guy. They have the two lovely girls, Kylie, who is off to university to study biology, you know, we are so pleased, and Sophie, who is so sweet and thoughtful when it comes to her old grandparents.'

'Mary, keep to the story, Sally has a job to do!'

'Yes, well, since we last met you they got divorced!'

Time for a shock-and-surprise look.

'No, really?'

'Yes, I know! It's quite sad, we are all upset. He decided to move to the countryside to run a new medical research centre. Well, I mean, after two kids you should take their needs into consid—'

'Mary…'

'Oh, sorry, Sally, I get carried away over that, not a nice business at all. Well, his company is sending him to a conference on a cruise ship. All expenses paid, you know! Very nice. But it's better than that. He can take the two girls with him. It'll be good for them to spend time together.'

'That's nice!'

Hush, Sally, don't interrupt, it will take much longer!

'Yes it is! He doesn't see them very much now. He lives miles from anywhere and they get bored visiting him. As you know, we don't come into town much these days. It's changed so much from when we were younger. All the new buildings. Gone are the shops we used to go to, now it's just a mall. It's a nice mall, but it's not like it used to be. And all the people! It was a nice quiet town, and now there are people from all over the world here, and so many people, and so much traffic. We are better off up the coast.

But today we have come down to meet up with them all before they set off tomorrow. They are staying here before they leave.'

'Yes. That's lovely, and exciting for them.' Hmm. That must be John's ship. It's the only cruise ship leaving in the next few days. 'We have a guest here at the moment who I think is working on that ship – his name is Mr Shedfield, and he is the guest services manager.'

'Oh, is he still here?'

I have no idea, I am still hoping he is.

'He checked out, but hasn't picked up his bags yet. I am sure your son-in-law and the girls will get to see plenty of him. Do tell them to pass on my regards.'

What did I just say? Why did I say that? I am normally very good at keeping guest confidentiality. Why did I feel the need to tell them about him?

'Well, if we don't see him we will tell them to look out for him. Remember, if you see our son-in-law, it's Dr Steven Hobart and girls, Kylie and Sophie.'

'Oh, sorry, I didn't realise it was Dr Hobart. They have already checked in!'

'That's great! We'll call them now.'

'Have a nice stay.'

I really wanted to say how nice the girls seemed, and Dr Hobart. But if I had then they would have started telling me how he might be nice for me, and gone on and on about it. I am not in the mood for that today! At least I now know he is divorced – I was right!

*

There goes Mrs Kirkstall, author of the most depressing cookbook in the world, off to meet her potential publisher. It would be interesting to read, and isn't that the problem? Even if you don't like the concept behind it, you would like to browse the book. If you saw it on a table you would pick it up. You couldn't help but do so. It'll probably have a sumptuous three-course meal on the cover, one that used up all those lonely single-person hours to prepare it, and you think, cooking for one? She'll probably get an amazing deal and then her own TV programme. I guess for some people that's how the world works. For me, no TV shows, no champagne book launches, just checking in and out. It's a shame I won't be here when she gets back, but I am sure she will tell me all about it tomorrow when she leaves!

*

That's a first – Maria passing out the back of the hotel with a ladder, and she's really struggling with it! I wonder what that's all about. I guess she probably needs it for something, maybe cleaning the hotel sign at the back, it's looked a mess since the wind yesterday blew leaves into it. Usually the window cleaners do that kind of thing. Odd, but Maria always surprises me.

*

Oh no, BW is back from his football interview – please don't come and annoy me with your ego! But hello, what has he dragged in with him? It's our favourite hooker. He better come quick as it's not long before we need the room back, he's only paid for it for the daytime. He's taking his time crossing the lobby, maybe he thinks we will see he has a 'fan'. We all know who she is, and last night she was with a woman, so don't think it's building up your masculinity in our eyes. Knowing her, she'll probably scare the shit out of you. The poor woman is unhappy – he's dawdling, doing that same slow walk with turns to the side. Hookers always walk in a direct line to the lifts, looking straight ahead. She'll probably look straight up at the bedroom roof too.

He's slowing her down. Maybe he wants his fan from earlier to come show her how famous he is. The guy would say, 'What a gentleman he is, and I met his lovely girlfriend too!'

Nobody knows her name, not even her 'business' name. She avoids everyone who works here. Well, I guess nobody is going to own up to using her services anyway. It's sad when someone doesn't have a name. It's like they are a ghost, they're not real, don't exist. One thing I will say is she dresses very normally, the colours coordinated simply. No bright 'red light' here – she is not at all tarty, quite inconspicuous. I guess that's deliberate so she can sneak in and out of the hotel unnoticed. She actually has no need to sneak, nobody will stop her. She is not part of the hotel, but some guests like her enough to be almost regulars. We never get complaints about her, even families don't recognise her for what she is. The police don't seem to notice, I assume if there are no complaints then there's no reason to. I wonder if Officer Hackness gets a 'discount' treat, and that's another reason he calls in so often. Maybe, in his mind, in his world of crime, he sees her as an undercover spy, rooting out suspicious behaviour for him. That's why she is left alone. Perhaps if this country was a dictatorship he would spy on everyone, even his friends, and report them as suspicious. Yes, I could see that.

*

Not too long before it's time to go home. Everything becomes such an effort by this time of the day, I'm exhausted and really need to get out of here now.

I wondered what happened to Miss Wilks and Mr Charles? No sign of them. I guess the police could have taken them out of the service exit. No Mr Temple about either. Can I tell Katie when she starts her shift or not? I bet he's the fall guy. The reason she has been randy with every man is to try get one to do her a 'favour' which results in them getting caught in the web of her deal. Maybe they both slipped out earlier without me noticing? Who knows if I'll ever see him again!

*

Did I just see that? It's the young couple who checked in at lunchtime. They just put their key in the express check-out! They came with no luggage, and although they booked for the night they seem to have decided to leave. People do use the express check-out to avoid leaving via reception – maybe they are shy, or embarrassed. I suppose they were here for a drink and sex only. It could be that they are not allowed to be together at home, for religious, cultural or family reasons. Although they

177

could be a couple having an affair or a hooker tryst, but at their age, and based on how attentive he was, more likely not.

'Maria, room 1507 is probably free, I don't think they are staying over.'

'Already? But isn't it booked until tomorrow?'

'Yes, Katie's on soon so she'll do the express check-outs and I am sure they dropped their key in it. Leave it for now, I'm just letting you know.'

'That's those two kids isn't it? Young people these days, terrible.'

'I'd say it's actually romantic. The parents are probably controlling and won't let them get together.'

'What? No, you should respect your parents. I am very traditional and don't like it if children disrespect their parents' wishes. Ha, mind you, if it was me...'

I wonder if you know all about that kind of thing, Maria.

*

Hurry up, Katie, the damned coach of tourists has arrived early and is unloading – let me out of here! I bet she has seen the line forming at the desk and found an excuse to slip off somewhere for a bit, then claim she knew nothing about it. Tourists used to be identifiable by someone with an umbrella or flag at the front of a line of people with big cameras around their necks. These days the queue looks more like a line of TV aerials. Selfie sticks bristling from all directions. This lot look like a furry caterpillar! Here's their guide, clipboard in hand!

178

'Hello, we're here.'

I can see that. He'll now get ready to address the perfectly formed line. The ones at the back won't be able to hear, and then they'll come to the front and mess it up. It'll be a scrum at the desk for the next hour. I don't know their language but, as with all groups, the guide feels the need to use some English to impress them. It pops out of the incomprehensible flow. I usually guess what the expression will be, each guide tends to use the same speech.

'Don't forget drink voucher!'

I can make out an echo rippling through the line of people practising saying it, ready to impress me with their skills. I'm used to it, I have coachloads like this every week. I'm actually quite relaxed when the chaos starts. I switch off and deal with whoever is in front of me until eventually the last one leaves. This time the names are OK – not back to front, in fact they even match their passports. Bet they won't next time.

'Selfie?'

Why do selfie stick holders always want posing shots with everything, even their food? I cannot imagine their friends are really that interested. It's my turn. Big smile.

'OK.'

Oh, no, others are pushing to the front to join in the same shot.

'Careful now.'

They are all over the place. I don't lose control of my desk. Nobody ever comes behind the desk.

'Maybe one at a time?'
'Ah! Accident!'

What just happened? He's the guide.

'Back from desk. Selfie later.'

'What happened?'

'Your certificate is destroyed, it was knocked onto the floor. So sorry.'

'My certificate? Oh, the notice!'

'Very sorry.'

'No, it's OK. But keep away from the glass.'

I feel a wonderful sense of release. I feel like I am floating on air. I am even enjoying walking all over the glass and notice as I continue to check them in. No time to clear it up – *crush*. Too many people to deal with just now – *crack*. Cleaning up will have to wait – *grind*.

'Don't forget drink voucher!'

'Oh, sorry, yes.'

I wish you had seen that, my missing flowers. It was a truly triumphant revenge. *Tip-tap*, *tip-tap*, hurrah! Here comes the cavalry!

'Sally, you are stood on a pile of glass!'

'Hi, Katie! Am I? Oh dear, the notice got knocked off by a tourist taking a selfie.'

Please let me enjoy this a little longer – *stamp*.

'Sally, clean it up and I'll finish off this lot!'

'OK. By the way, the football player Brad Wicklane is upstairs with our usual hooker. He only has the room for the day so he shouldn't be long! Alas, no hooker game to be played tonight!'

'Yes, Alex mentioned seeing them come in when I arrived! Maybe she'll be back later – plenty of time for another punter!'

CHAPTER 12

TIME TO GO HOME!

'So, flowers – and, vase, you too – I miss you.'

I find myself talking to an empty space on the desk, and it's an empty life for me. Losing one of my best friends, I'll have nobody to confide in all day. For the animals it'll no longer be only exotic trips, they will have to listen to all of my work stories now, but only when I get home. It's so sad I never got to say goodbye to you. As each flower was replaced in the vase I'd say goodbye to it. I knew which ones that so-called florist would remove. Some of you I removed myself, to put you out of your misery. The desk feels unbalanced now, and I feel unstable.

Shame about John – creep that he is, it may have been nice to see him. It will be a long day tomorrow: a rush of tourists then the cruise ship people checking out. They'll get to play with John for a couple of weeks. Most likely he'll get to play with at least one of them!

'Goodnight, my dear, lost flowers.'

My homework tonight is an easy exercise: changing a light bulb! It's one thing having energy-efficient ones, but why, with all the modern technology, do they ever need replacing? Maybe we are not as advanced a species as we think we are. Of course, by now I have a big selection at home in a storage box, mainly due to buying the wrong size, power or fitting! But Sally has now graduated from college with a diploma in light bulbs, and now I know all the different types for my sockets.

After my lovely romantic trip to Italy with the cat yesterday, I am starving again after only having a salad at lunchtime because of that stupid John. Tonight the tiger and I are going to have adventures in India! Indian beer is well known, and I should drink that. But I prefer wine to beer. It doesn't bloat me up like beer, and I can enjoy my food without feeling too full. I also have memories of my youth. Boys would drink beer and then burp in my face, laughing, as if it was funny. The smelly breath when they would try kiss me. I associate beer with bad, not good times. Wine is more refined. Alas, I cannot find Indian wine in my supermarket so beer it will have to be, just a small bottle. There are so many types of curry you can have. There are some nice varieties in the supermarket these days, not just something called *mild*, *medium* or *hot*. Best of all, you only have to microwave them! I know this is cheating, but after Mrs Kirkstall, the 'food for one' woman, I refuse to fill up my evening cooking everything from scratch! The tiger and I will watch a Bollywood musical. They are so colourful and everyone is either happy or tragically sad, and even if I get confused over what's happening it does not matter!

I'm feeling really sad about the flowers and John. Tonight, the tiger and I will forget everything on our magical trip to India. The tiger will enjoy the smells of my cooking – well, heating-up, anyway. The music and dancing in the film will

182

make it feel really at home. Although tigers do eat people, it will get to sit on the sofa with me tonight and watch the film, provided it's well behaved! Grrr!

Now, a quick check in the mirror. Yes, Sally is presentable enough for the commute home. It's 3pm and I'm out of here. Shop, take off make-up, drink, read a magazine, eat in front of the TV, bed, egg in nest, try to sleep.

I feel so empty. I feel like I have lost someone close twice in one day. The flowers, tragically, and even, though I never got to know him, John. I was ready for him, and now nothing. I guess tomorrow will be yet another red-and-black checked ribbon day. I'm sure I'll be fine.

WEDNESDAY

CHAPTER 13

GOOD MORNING!

'Good morning, mirror!'

Life returns to normal. Yes, it's yet another red-and-black checked ribbon day! Red nail polish, black panties and black tights. Not a spotty or stripy day. Just another square old day, alas.

'Good morning, empty space.'

No little girl today. No flowers in their vase. I wonder what Lily will be doing now. She's probably just about to be dropped off at the childminder's. I wonder if she is talking to the flowers there? Surely there will be plants and flowers at a childminder's? Children have to know what nature is – touch her, smell her, embrace her, hear her and love her. It's not just about seeing nature on a display screen or in a book. Nature should impact all your senses; that's why we humans have senses in the first place! Maybe the miserably politically correct in disguise as health and safety people banned vases of flowers at childminders' premises, seeing them as a hazard. Maybe that's why Lily enjoyed seeing them here. I bet the PC types would demand the vase be screwed down, and claim flowers were a choking hazard. Scaring people with the deadly consequences of toppling over. Like you suffered, my friends.

'Good morning, Matt!'

'Hi, Sally. I don't look as good as usual without the flowers on the desk!'

'Don't be silly. But I know what you mean.'

I miss you, flowers, the space really does look empty without you. I'll miss gossiping about the events of the day and, of course, the cheesy chat-ups! At least you don't have to suffer the smell of my breath after a lovely trip with the tiger to India last night! I've tried everything I can think of, but I am sure the spices are still lingering.

'I hope Mr Temple doesn't think that notice can go back on the desk now!'

'I've not heard anything about that, it's an office thing. But guess what?'

Roll-the-eyes time.

'What?'

'Big drama yesterday late afternoon!'

'Oh, what was it?'

'Apparently Mr Charles was taken away by the police yesterday, not long after you left. Katie said he looked very scared and pale, as if in shock! Who would have thought someone who was a long-standing customer would get into trouble?'

Not 'customer'; he's a guest!

'He was more likely worried about potentially not getting his hotel loyalty points, that's probably why he looked like that!'

Gosh, how strange, did I make a joke? John would have been impressed. But why did I say that? I am so used to suppressing what I am thinking. I don't want to get into trouble. I'm feeling a little scared, nervous. Am I losing my self-control? Is something happening to me?

'Ha-ha! Katie also mentioned that Mr Temple had taken all the express check-out room keys and made a real mess trying to work out which was for which room – took her ages to do the check-outs.'

He laughed at my joke, well, sort of, enough of a laugh. Maybe it is better not to tell a joke and just let humour come out naturally like John said. I am worried. What if I tell one again and it causes problems, like with the professor? Maybe I just got away with that one. I don't know what's best to do. Should I mention about Miss Wilks? I'm not sure if I'm allowed to.

'Was anyone else involved?'

'Nobody. Oh, apparently Miss Wilks won't be bothering Peter the barman today as she has checked out. But guess what? Her credit card turned out to be an illegal copy of someone else's! Apparently the card owner checked her statement online when she discovered it was out of credit. It was the hotel pre-authorisation the owner knew nothing about!'

'Oh dear.'

Maybe I'm the only one who knows she may be implicated. Maybe Miss Wilks left because the card had stopped working, so fled as soon as she realised. Maybe she is naughty, but it looks like Mr Charles really has done something wrong.

'I can't wait for Officer Hackness to come in for his coffee later this morning!'

Mind you, if he is like he was yesterday I'm wasting my time.

'See ya!'

'Bye.'

Let's look at the night log. Oh, a note from Katie – the florist will replace the flowers this morning. I bet she will come when I'm not around. It's nice someone thought to organise that without me asking. I wonder who? Probably Mr Temple, who will have whinged at the cost of a new vase! Katie may have said something to him, but he acted quickly. Maybe it's all about the need for flowers at reception, nothing to do with me at all. I suppose the flowers, like me, would not be missed, just replaced. Ah well, I guess that's to be expected.

I feel the same emptiness as the vacant space where the flowers and vase used to be. I feel more loss over those flowers than my family. Is that right or fair to say? It's how I feel. When my parents or brother die, how will I react? Like I do over the flowers? Probably not as strongly. I never see them or talk to them on the Internet. I don't think I have any residual feeling for them at all. I, or maybe they, lost that years ago. Of course, I may have something somewhere deep inside that would come out later, but I don't think so. I could imagine that the loss of a boyfriend or partner would be horrific, especially as finding the right person is so difficult. Maybe it's better not to be in any relationship with something that could die, it's all too painful a prospect. I have my stuffed animals, they don't die, they just wear out a bit. The flowers change, but I was used to that, and when they die they create compost and are reborn, so never really lost. Of course, and I won't forget this, the space in front of me now is effectively due to murder, not a natural cycle. That is very hard to take.

That's nice. The Hobarts and their grandparents are going into breakfast together. The girls still with their music on. Harry and Mary keep turning to talk to them, and then Dr Hobart has to tell them to take their earphones out! As usual, they just take one out, then go back to listening. Has talking to your grandchildren been interrupted by technology? I bet they are happy to chat via the Internet, but face-to-face, oh no, that's so retro! Unless retro is in fashion again, of course.

I wonder if I'll ever get to play grandmother? Would I want to? Have the grandchildren dumped on me whenever the parents can't be bothered entertaining them, need a break or want to do something without them. Since my parents aren't around I couldn't do that myself if I had a child. I guess I'd have to make sure the father had parents who lived near enough, and long enough, to dump the kids on!

*

Yesterday I put Mrs Jackson in 1308, the whinger room. Surprisingly, she has not complained at all during her stay. Katie and Matt have put nothing in the overnight log about her. Maybe she was so tired after her oh-so-stressful trip that she slept all day! She's due to check out later this morning. I just hope she isn't bottling it all up and about to explode over me! Once again, Sally at reception will get the shit for everything and everybody in the hotel. I wouldn't be surprised if she complains about the other guests too. I can imagine her saying the guests are not like the ones at home!

*

Mrs Kirkstall is heading this way, still in her hippy clothes from yesterday. I cannot understand why so many people don't have fresh clothes every day. It is so unhygienic and smelly. I can imagine her cooking at home is equally messy.

'Good morning, Mrs Kirkstall! How did it go yesterday?'

'Good morning. I am not sure. They didn't like my title.'

'Oh dear.'

'Well, I wanted it to represent the idea behind the book, so thought *Lonely Night Banquets*. But they think other keywords like sumptuous are important! But I don't want it it to sound like any other cookbook.'

It probably is to them.

'Did they like your recipes?'

'Oh, they didn't seem overly interested in them, but we did chat about their ideas on the kind of photos to use, especially for the cover.'

I guess, to them, that's what sells cookbooks. The content is less important. I doubt they ever use a cookbook themselves. Probably only the microwave, or heating something up in an oven! I reckon they all eat out on expenses and have takeaways. Sounds like they never actually read your book.

'I am sure the recipes are lovely. I will look out for it when it comes out. When is it likely to be at the bookstore?'

'They said about a year from now, they are very busy.'

192

'So they will publish it?'

'Well, to be honest I didn't really understand much about what was going on. They seemed so vague about everything.'

They are probably being polite and thinking, *No, we'll reject her 'after some consideration' by email.*

'I wish you luck!'

'Thank you, I better check out now, got to get back home!'

CHAPTER 14

HOW WAS YOUR STAY?

Oops, flashing light.

'Sally at reception, how can I help you?'

'It's Mr Smith in room 1405. Can you ask the concierge to collect our bags?'

'Of course, I'll do it right away.'

I feel sympathetic towards Mrs Smith today. Imagine how hard it must be for her.

'Alex, Mr and Mrs Smith in 1405 need their bags collecting.'

'She seemed such a cow when she checked in, and didn't tip me for the airport transfer. I'm not sure I want to help her. Plus, I have all these tourist group bags to shift to the coach, and that's before the cruise lot check out.'

You shouldn't expect a tip every bloody time, and the transfer company probably give you commission anyway. You keep claiming you don't get any when I know you do.

'Please do it now. Let's try and check them out before the tourists get in line.'

Groan. Here come the foreign tourist group. I got out of checking most of them in, but now I need help, where's Frank?

Oh, Mrs Smith is now in the line.

'Mrs Smith, if you are ready to check out, just drop your key in the express check-out box.'

She's not looking at me. Well, unless one of them sees me they'll have to wait.

'Selfie, yes?'

Oh no, here we go again.

'OK, but quick, there are many people to check out!'

I know they didn't understand a word I said, but at least I said it. Damn, they are all coming forward at once.

'Ouch!'

Who said that?

'That woman has a dog in her bag. My wife just went to pat it and it bit her!'

Please, Frank, help!

*

Look who's here: that so-called florist!

'Hello, Sally, I have the replacement flowers and vase. Shall I put them where you had the previous ones?'

Fake a light smile.

'Yes.' Don't expect me to say anything more. Oh no, the vase is all wrong. 'The vase is not the same.'

'Yes, unfortunately they don't make the old one any more. This is the new model, more fashionable, similar colour.'

'But I liked the old one. Why did they change the design?'

'We all have to keep up with the times, don't we, Sally?'

195

Don't 'Sally' me, you bitch. How you can be called a florist I have no idea. You know nothing about flowers. Look at her, she's brought a bloody mixed bunch! The colours don't go together at all, how awful. Now, see how she is arranging the flowers: standing back, looking at them, reaching to pull one out, standing back, putting it back in, standing back, time and time again. She has no idea what she is doing. She just wants to appear professional.

'There we are. Bye, Sally.'

Fake smile. You won't get a 'Bye' from me. I can feel myself frowning at the new vase and flowers. It's good there are no guests at the desk, Sally doesn't frown in public. I don't know what to say to the flowers. I am used to one or two changes in the vase, but not all at once. I usually have a few familiar friends around after the florist has been. This time I feel shy. But it's their first day, maybe they feel the same. I wonder if they all know each other – which of us is the new kid in class? But they are a mixed bunch, the poor flowers will get confused over their meaning. All flower displays should have a meaning, a message in their colours. I'll have to sort them out, take the yellows to the office. Keep the pinks, reds and purples here. I won't say a thing. The florist never talks to them, so maybe it is better I don't, not yet. Let them and the new vase settle in a bit before I introduce myself. I feel nervous, like I am about to go on a first date.

*

'Hi, Sally, your espresso macchiato! I see the florist has brought you new flowers!'

You would. She is attractive, but shit as a florist.

'Yes, the vase is different, and the flowers need rearranging.'

'Did you hear about Mr Charles?'

Peter the gossip strikes again. I'm not giving anything away.

'What?'

'The police arrested him. I suspect it's to do with that Miss Wilks. I think I had a really lucky escape there!'

I know more than you, but I'm saying nothing.

'I'm hoping Officer Hackness has something more to say about it when he comes for his coffee.'

I reckon Officer Hackness listens to gossip, but says nothing. Now I know why he goes to the bar each day – not just to see me, but to listen to your stories!

*

I wonder how many hours I have spent looking into you, mirror? Think of all the people who have looked into you, all the stories you could tell. When people look in a mirror they think about how they look, what impression they are giving to the world, true or false. They say walls have ears and can remember everything, but I think mirrors hold much deeper, darker secrets. Oh, what is Brad Wicklane doing here coming out of the lift today? He should have checked out yesterday afternoon! Here he comes. I'd better pretend I didn't see anything when he came in with the hooker. Although it really looked like he wanted everyone to notice.

'Mr Wicklane, what a surprise to see you!'

'I am surprising, Sally! You should watch me play!'

I think you actually meant that. It wasn't a joke. You are a jerk, and not even a funny jerk. Just a plain old jerk.

'Ah, I can see you have extended your stay to today.'

'Yes, your football team were so pleased with me they invited me back this morning to meet some of the players!'

Bullshit, it was probably for the hooker. Ah, yes, here she comes, out of the lift and heading straight out. Her usual method of having her clients distract the reception staff as she slips out.

'Excellent, I am so pleased for you.'

'Yes, so I need to check out and get over there!'

It's so funny when guests come up with stories to tell while she slips away. Some really struggle. Lying is not for everyone. But it is for Brad. Maybe as you fade in your career you feel more pressure to exaggerate the truth, struggling to try to maintain an image. Rather than accept your best days are over, and approach it professionally, some just have to lie, risk taking drugs to keep going or whatever. He's a whatever. Nice body, though.

*

Oh good, a check-out from the cruise ship. I'm beginning to get worried about them waiting until the last minute. Dr Karlsen has such a lovely, natural way of walking. You would think she was on a catwalk as she sways through the lobby.

'Good morning, Dr Karlsen, how can I help you?'

'Good morning. Do you have any messages for me?'

198

'Let me see. Nothing in the card box, but let me check the computer. Yes, there is a message from someone called Brandon. It says he will be in the bar early today.'

'OK, thank you.'

Off she goes, the eyes of the lobby following her. I'd love to talk with the flowers about how I feel, but it's too soon. They need to settle in a bit first. Brandon is not that common a name around here, is it? And the bar? It must be the same guy who came in on Monday, following those people looking for Mr Akkad. If he's a private detective maybe she is a client of his. I cannot imagine she would have any other reason to have anything to do with him. It's not like he's particularly intelligent or attractive!

Now I am beginning to feel jealous of her again! Over Dr Karlsen and Brandon, but I hardly know him, and I don't find him particularly interesting. Brandon! This really pisses me off. Who do I blame? John for being understanding, Dr Karlsen for being attractive, or myself? Maybe John has awoken something in me that has been suppressed for years. This is really, really annoying. I don't do jealousy. You cannot control feeling jealous, if you feel it you feel it, it is soul-destroying. That's one reason I avoid relationships.

Mirror! Do I look the jealous type? Surely not! Could I look like Dr Karlsen? Surely not! Oh, and bugger, she obviously isn't checking out yet.

*

There's old Mr Turner and his young wife and child, all dressed up to go out, in fact very smart-casual, not just normal smart-casual. The young daughter even has make-up on at this time of the morning. I wonder if Mrs Turner is the one who's fussy about dress and behaviour. Ah, they are coming to see me.

'Good morning! How can I help you today, Mr Turner?'

'Do we have time for breakfast? We were a little late getting up and we wanted something before we go to the zoo.'

Two women with make-up to do, clothes to be tried on and discarded, and only one bathroom mirror. It's always a recipe for disaster, and delays! I bet they told him half a dozen times they were 'nearly ready, darling'!

'Breakfast is over by now, but if you go in I am sure the buffet will not have been cleared away yet. You can always get coffee and a roll at the bar if they have cleared it.'

'Thank you.'

That's nice, somebody has said thank you to me for a change! Why would the young girl wear make-up to go to the zoo? I only wear full make-up for work, and only a little when going out somewhere. It's too much effort, and my skin needs to breathe. It's part of calming down after work, taking off the make-up and changing into relaxing clothes. Maybe Mummy treats the girl like a doll to dress and make up. The girl seems happy enough. I could see Mrs Turner as one of those pageant mums you see on TV. Although she's not the pushy type, I reckon she could be really, really stubborn.

Why do I feel nervous? All I need to do is say hello to the flowers. It's their first day and they may be as nervous as I am. I'd better not say why I am moving some of their friends to the office, they may get upset. They could have been together for a while. I don't want them thinking I am some kind of flower racist, but certain colours in a vase go together, and some don't. Also, it's not a good idea to mention about the new vase. Even if I don't like it, it's probably the only real vase they have known and they may be proud of it.

'Hello, my new flowers!'

Sorry for not talking to you earlier, but I wasn't sure what to say! My name is Sally, and we are here at reception in the hotel. I am sure we will become good friends, and have a lot to talk about! We will see a lot of strange things here at reception. Your friends here, who I am now moving to the office, will have fun too, but here is very different.

*

Well, it's after ten o'clock and all is not well! Where is Officer Hackness? I want to know what's happening with Mr Charles and Miss Wilks. Oh, here he comes, maybe he had a longer-than-usual chat with Alex the concierge. I can imagine Alex pumping him for information. He looks his normal self today.

'Hello, Sally, I see I've caught you at a quiet moment.'

'No, not really, I think the tide is out before a tsunami hits! I have a group of cruise ship passengers and I am worried they will all come down to check out at the same time.'

Cruise ship, water, tsunami. I made another joke! Wow! But he doesn't seem to have got my sense of humour.

'I'm a little late today as I had a bit of paperwork to finish after yesterday. You were a great help, Sally. However, I need to ask a few questions in private. Can we go into the office for a second? Nobody is in there.'

'Yes, they are on a training programme this morning.' Funny how the whole office can just disappear! 'I can only be a minute, I am not supposed to leave the desk. Remember, I am waiting for a tsunami!'

A second chance for you to get it, crack a smile.

'Tsunamis are not things to joke about, Sally.'

Oh no, he's a bloody politically correct type! There's no hope of a relationship with you then, not with funny girl Sally! John would have got it. Even if his response was only half a smile and a 'ha-ha', some appreciation is better than nothing.

So, here we are in the office and he automatically takes the best seat, clears the desk in front of him and then invites me to sit down. Total control freak.

'Sally, it seems your Mr Charles and Miss Wilks were collaborating. From what you could tell, would that seem reasonable to say?'

'I thought they were sleeping together.'

With his lack of humour I am not going to mention headmistresses and canes!

'Did they know each other before they arrived?'

'I don't know. They met at the bar and went out together at lunchtime the day before yesterday. What's that beeping?' *Beep, beep, beep.*

'It sounds like the Internet is playing up. Well, if we need to know more I'll let you know.'

That it? I feel like he just wanted an excuse to get me alone, but he asked nothing personal. I assume he's in a rush now as he's missing his fix of coffee.

'The Internet?'

'Yes, that box over there controls the Internet for the hotel. It beeps when there is a problem on the line, usually a supplier issue.'

'Supplier issue?'

'The company that provides the Internet connection. Usually any problem is with them, not the box itself. If you turn it off and on it'll fix itself. Look, let me show you. See, all the lights are now off, no Internet. Now I'll switch it back on, just wait a second or two and, there we are, all the lights are back on, it's working again! The beeping has stopped now, so it must have been a temporary fault which turning it off and on has cleared.'

He is smiling triumphantly, as if I should be really impressed with his knowledge. But he didn't smile at my joke, so no big, amazed Sally grin from me.

'Oh. Does it work the Wi-Fi too?'

'Yes, Sally. But you must get back to your desk.'

Interesting.

*

Why does my heart sink every time the boss appears in the lobby? Management never come to my desk to make compliments, it's always to dump some problem on me to clear up.

'Mr Temple, good afternoon.'

'Good morning, you mean!'

Shit, am I that nervous? Maybe all the excitement of Mr Charles has got to me. Oh no, he's carrying the bloody notice in a new frame, another old-fashioned gold one! Has he no imagination? At least think what design would look best in the lobby, match the decor.

'We wouldn't want our customers confused, would we now?'

Guests! Is that a real half-smile or a sarcastic smile? Maybe he thinks he's being funny, it's hard to tell.

'Of course not.'

'How are the flowers?'

'Lovely, thank you for getting them replaced so quickly. The desk feels almost back to normal. It's a shame about the vase, it had been here as long as I have.'

'And that's some time, GSA, isn't it?'

Sally, I am called Sally, say Sally! In any case, it's bad grammar to say 'GSA', so use my name, you shit. Read my badge. The flowers get called by their name, why not me? I'm surprised you didn't call them an RFD, reception flower display, or something stupid like that.

'I like it here.'

Come on, what about the notice, why are you holding it?

'So, I have decided it is safer to have the notice put up on the wall behind you. We wouldn't want guests hurt by breaking glass if it fell over again, would we?'

And what about me?

'I wonder, maybe it's not big enough to be read by someone stood at reception. We may need to get a larger one. In the meantime, can you get maintenance to put it up for you?'

For me? Put it up for me? Does he not listen?

'Of course.'

And no way will there be another, bigger one.

'That, my new flowers, was Mr Temple.'

He is the big boss, and we have to do what he says. Well, rather, as you will see, we have to make sure he thinks we have done what he says. He called you flowers! You are lucky, in his world I don't have a name, I am a GSA. Not even Sally the GSA.

Despite that chat with Mr Temple, my world feels like it's returning to normal. Now I have the flowers to talk to, it's a great help. Although I have all these people around me, I had nobody to confide in. I'd better call Bill. It was interesting that Mr Temple called Bill 'maintenance' like he's a whole department, although there is only one of him. No initials of a job title for Bill. Maybe when they recruited him they told him he would run a department, but not that he would be it, in its entirety!

'Hello, this is Sally at reception. Mr Temple would like you to come and put up a notice on the wall by my desk as soon as possible.'

No, flowers, he was not there, what did you expect? But did you see what I did? Rather than ask him myself, I said Mr Temple wants it done. If he has a problem taking orders from women, this should mean it gets done. Mind you, I hate the notice so I really don't care if it stays on the floor!

*

Here comes Ed with another delivery.

'So, what brings Santa to Sally today?'

205

'There's nobody in the office!'

'They are on a training programme this morning.' He has not realised I have a new vase and flowers! 'Notice anything different?'

'Err, nope.'

'I have a new vase of flowers!'

'Oh. Anyway, got to go!'

Is that it? Someone killed my flowers and you can only say, 'Oh', not even 'Oh!' If a guy loves a woman he recognises the little things. In this case it's a big thing. John notices the little things in my life. You just want sex, and so does John but at least he remembers things!

'I'm sorry, flowers!'

It's not your fault he didn't notice you. I am happy to introduce you to people, but he is just so full of himself he sees nothing around him!

*

Oh, why is Mr Temple coming over here again so soon?

'Mr Temp—'

'Have you seen this Internet review?'

'What?'

'*This is the worst hotel in the entire world I have ever stayed in!*'

'Who wrote that?'

'It doesn't say, who's in 1308? They say, *never stay in room 1308!* She was here last night, apparently. She was checked in after a long journey by some *inconsiderate, unsympathetic and downright rude woman* at reception.'

Oh shit! I can feel myself starting to go numb. I feel sick. What? I need to clear my head.

'Let me look.' I am so scared. I don't know why, but I am. 'It's Mrs Jackson. She was put in 1308 as it's our whing…'

Oops, he doesn't know about that.

'Our what?'

'Whinger room.' No, no, why did I blurt it out? 'It's the room we use for guests who are most likely to complain. It doesn't seem right to put them in a nice room as they will complain anyway.'

'What? What kind of logic is that? You put the most upset guests in the worst room? No wonder this kind of disaster happens!'

Don't raise your voice to me! Now I am getting angry, not upset.

'She's still here, well, unless she used express checkout.'

How the hell could she have the nerve to write that whilst still here? What kind of person would do that? She probably couldn't face me and has gone.

'Call her room, if she's there, say that the hotel manager would like to address her concerns.'

'What? How can I call her after she said that about me?'

'Call her. And apologise for your attitude yesterday!'

'I didn't have an attitude yesterday, she is just a miserable type of person who moans all the time about everything.'

'That may well be, but this looks really bad!'

'OK, but she is due to check out this morning, so can I wait until then?'

'No, now, I want it taken off the Internet.'

I feel like crap. He's standing there watching. I think he enjoys this power over me. Why's he not on my side? Maybe he is enjoying watch me suffer, gets off on it in some cruel way.

'She's not answering.'

'Keep trying.'

Good, he's gone.

'Flowers, you shouldn't see that kind of thing on your first day. I am so sorry.'

I actually rang a vacant room. Maybe Frank can deal with her. I can't face the bitch.

*

That's nice – the Turners look a lot better for having breakfast. The food must have done them good, they look like a family now. She has her arm under his and the young daughter is actually looking at them and talking, probably about what they will see at the zoo. Mind you, Mrs Turner generally seems quite distant from Mr Turner. As if she is going through the motions of the relationship rather than fully embracing it. If they have been married a long time maybe she has got bored. But if he's no longer interesting to her, maybe she just switches off. She'd better watch out, it won't be long before she is starting to fantasise about things to fill the void.

*

OK, now it's time to see how the check-outs are going. Oh no, they are not! What? Nearly all the cruise people are still in their rooms. I don't mind being busy, but all at once would be too much. A tsunami, even. Yes, I am funny, even if Officer Hackness thinks I have bad taste.

'Hello, Sally.'

'John!'

Oh damn, did I say or shout that? Do I look confused? Am I blushing through my make-up? I can feel it melting under the heat!

'I see you are wearing the same bow as when we first met!'

I feel faint, dizzy. At least he's talking, my mouth is temporarily out of action. I do get that you notice my bow now, so you can chill about that. Where do I look? I can't look at him! Shit, this isn't cool at all.

'I also see you have a new flower vase. Why did you change it? This is OK, but I rather liked the other one.'

A question – oh, what pressure. Come on, mouth, brain, connect!

'Err, well, it had an accident.'

'Shame, but at least you have moved the notice over by the wall there. Much better, I say, but why's it on the floor?'

'It's waiting to be put up by the maintenance guy, but there's no sign of him so I left a message. Do men have a problem taking orders from women?'

'Sally, that's a very out-of-date view! If he was sexist he probably would want to be around you whilst he was doing the job, even starting quickly and making it last as long as he could stretch it out. Sally, you are very attractive, you know that don't you?'

What? Where did that come from? How did he manage to turn the discussion into how I look? This is too much to handle, I feel flustered. This is not me – I am normal, boring, nothing really. I have to ignore what he said.

'Do you have maintenance people on your boat?'

'It's a ship, Sally, a bit bigger than a boat!'

Don't correct me, you are going backwards in my estimation here. Just ride with my mistakes, don't make me feel small. Don't criticise me unless I am really, really bad. You are so close to getting what you want, and maybe what I want, but the way you said that one sentence is freaking me out.

'Our maintenance guy cannot find his ladder, and left his toolbox somewhere.'

'Sorry, Sally, did I say something wrong? You sound more serious.'

Thank you, and yes. But how do I answer that?

'It's nothing really.'

'Really? Come on, tell me.'

No, no, no. Shut up. It's bad enough making a mistake, but don't go over the top trying to make it right. You are going to dig us both into a hole we might never get out of. Just let's get on with maintenance.

'Forget it. Anyway, the notice can stay there as far as I am concerned. It can get swept away by housekeeping, assuming they can find their brushes!'

He's smiling, a nice smile, good, the pressure is off.

'Very funny!'

You understand me. You are so much like me. We like the same things. You are so perfect! Stop now! You don't even know him. He's in guest relations. He's like a salesman. You never know what they really think as they spend their lives

210

trying to make you feel comfortable and then manipulate you.

'Yes, I am much happier it's off the desk.'

'It seems quieter than usual today!'

'It's your group for the cruise. They are all likely to come down at the last minute, a tsunami!'

'Flood down, will they?'

Hurrah, he made a joke too! 'Stream, even!' What a lovely smile. Oh, I am enjoying this. 'They all seem to be doctors.'

'Yes, it's a medical conference. In fact, I am here to see the organiser, Mr Akkad.'

What? You are seeing him? This is so strange.

'Really?'

'He called me in to sort out some special arrangements for the guests.'

'Have you ever met him?'

'No, why do you ask?'

'He looks a bit like an old-fashioned gangster. I'm just warning you.'

'Thank you, Sally. Got to go, see you later!'

I hope so, but it's my lunch break soon. Now I feel emotionally drained, but somehow elated. I have to change my ribbon and get out of these tights. I cannot feel like I want to feel when I'm dressed like this! He saw that the flowers have changed, but I know it's his job to notice changes in everything. That's part of the guest service function. I even comment when someone changes clothes, handbag, shoes. Often they have been shopping in the mall and I'm the first person they get to show. They like the fact I notice.

So, I must not let myself think he is interested in me, really interested in me. He appears really interested in everybody he meets. But I'm not sure. Why do I always look on the negative side of things?

Let's look, mirror, how bad do I look after that emotional roller coaster? Am I blushing through my make-up? Not now, but I must have been then. At least it didn't run, as far as I can tell.

'My new flowers, that was Mr Shedfield, John.'

He isn't normally in a suit, he looks very smart. I was surprised to see him like that. Light grey isn't my idea of a nice suit. I like men in dark colours, almost black, then they look more like a film star! But in grey he'd make a handsome groom, don't you think? Well, assuming he is not married of course. Oh shit. I don't know, do I? I forgot to find out! I always assume men who chat me up are married unless proven otherwise. I've been so focused on him I forgot all about a possible partner. Damn, damn, damn. Is it too late to find out? How do I raise the subject? Now I feel all flustered, in a panic!

*

I wonder why Maria is calling. I'm the one who usually calls her!

'Maria!'

'Nobody is leaving their rooms! How do you expect us to do housekeeping if people stay in their rooms?'

'Yes, I am guessing they'll all come down about the same time to get their bus. I'm struggling to think of something to get them moving.'

'But they know we have a check-out time!'

'Yes, but we can't stop them all coming at once! It's the same with all the tour groups, they come down for breakfast then sit in their rooms until the last minute. It's really annoying!'

'You must do something, I have never known it to be this bad!'

'I'm off for lunch now, so hopefully things will be moving by the time I come back.'

I doubt it. This lot are obsessed with their computers, checking their emails, chatting, sending photos! Intelligent people they may be, well, educated at least, but their technology addiction is like kids with toys, they won't let go!

CHAPTER 15

LUNCHTIME!

'Well, it's time for lunch, my new flowers!'

I go every day at this time to lunch. I have a routine for my lunches and dinners, which I'll explain in more detail later. You have a lot to take in on your first day at work, so I'll spread the details out over a few days. Don't worry, I'll be back soon!

It's too soon to discuss personal stuff and chat-ups with the flowers. They need to settle in a bit first. I'll explain about that to them later. But I need to work out what to do about John's marital status. I could ask him directly – he can only say yes or no. It wouldn't surprise me if he's divorced. It must be so tempting to have an affair in his job, away weeks at a time with attractive women all around him. I could just slip the words 'your wife' into the conversation and see how he responds. I'll have to make sure I think of something to say that will let me do that. Maybe his wife chose his suit? Groan.

I am excited seeing John today, and feel closer than ever to him. I do hope he is still here when I get back. Even though the Indian meal last night was very filling, especially with beer, seeing John has given me an appetite. So, today is a sandwich day! That's my really hungry lunch.

Quick look in the mirror. Hmm, presentable, but it's definitely not a red and black check day after all! I can't talk to John looking like this. I need to pick up some pink panties, I want to feel girlie. I won't have time today to change my nail varnish, but I must change into some hold-ups. It's time for a nice red-and-pink spotty bow. That will put me in the right frame of mind.

*

What do you think, mirror? A perfect bow. Teeth brushed, make-up restored, no stains on clothing. Good. Here we go, only four hours and I'm out of here. What a sweet girlie I am now! I am ready for John.

'Hi, flowers! I'm back, as I promised!'

Notice the change in ribbon? I have a nice red-and-pink spotty bow.

CHAPTER 16

GOOD AFTERNOON!

At last, Bill the maintenance guy is in the lobby. He's coming over, it's as if he's been waiting for me.

'Sally, you were out when I arrived.'

Why did he wait for me? Frank could have dealt with it. Maybe Bill avoids management, he would have had to get on with the job. If it's good old Sally he can take advantage of my nature. It's possible he wants to be around me, as John suggested could happen. Whatever, no doubt he came because I mentioned it was a Mr Temple request.

'It's over there, leaning against the wall.'

'Hmm. Well, I'll need my ladder and toolbox for that, I better go try and find them.'

Do I shout at him, and say, 'You have spent the whole day looking for your ladder'?

'My new flowers, do you think I am too soft?'

I guess you haven't known me long enough to have much of an opinion. Mirror, do I look like I could be a naughty girl? Yes, I am in a red-and-pink spotty bow, a racy combination, I know. Hardly anyone on the cruise has checked out. I am going to turn off the Internet. That'll get them down! Wait, wait, wait, what am I thinking? Is it hormones? I feel like some kind of terrorist plotting to do something terrible.

'Yes!'

Where did that come from?

'Oh, Maria! I didn't notice you there, did I think aloud?'

'No, I have rooms to get ready! What are you going to do about it?'

'We have a group of veteran cricketers arriving later and it would not go down well if the press heard that famous names of the past could not get a room when they arrived! Maybe I should turn off the Wi-Fi, I'm sure that would get them down here quickly. Where is Frank? I ought to ask his permission. He's never around when needed!'

'Just do it!'

'OK.'

Here we go. Naughty Sally. Into the empty office. I feel like a thief, stealing the Internet! Take a deep breath. Turn off the box as Officer Hackness explained. The crime is committed. Now I'd better get back to the desk!

'Well?'

'Maria, I did it. I took down the World Wide Web with one push of a button!'

Nothing, deathly silence.

'Do you think it's always like this when you commit a crime? A silence and stillness after the big build-up? It's like nothing happened, surely someone will complain.'

'They'll probably be trying to reconnect. They are so used to losing connections or slow speeds with the hotel Wi-Fi.'

Come on, the suspense is killing me!

'Here we go, Maria, the telephone flashing has started.

I'm not answering. Look, the lift is moving too. You better get to your battle stations, a lot of rooms to deal with!'

It's pale-faced Nicole from reservations heading this way, but out though the lifts comes my tsunami, so she'll have to wait. She's washed away by the tide to the bar for her coffee. No, that was not as funny. Maybe I should try to be humorous about something else!

Oops, Nicole is back quickly and I am busy with a line of people now. Please don't interrupt me. I have my job to do, and you would hate it if I interrupted you doing yours. Everyone thinks they can just butt in, but it's rude. I know it's easier interrupting when I have someone in front of me than when I'm on the phone. You can see when there is a pause in the conversation and strike. If someone's on a phone you don't know if the other person is talking. But surely, talking face-to-face to people is more important than via a phone!

'Sally, sorry to interrupt, but any idea what's happened to the Internet? The reservations system has crashed, and we were doing a software update at the same time. It's a disaster!'

Why do people always say they are sorry to interrupt when they are not?'

'No, have you asked the office staff?'

'There is nobody in there, and I have no idea how to deal with this.'

'It's probably just a supplier issue. I'm sure it will be back on soon.'

Go back to your box of a room and leave me alone. I really sound like I know what I am talking about – 'supplier issue': thank you, Officer Hackness, for that.

'I hope so. Mr Temple is going to be furious.'

What's new? He's always upset over something!

*

Oh, here comes John! Stay calm, look natural. Don't give anything away.

'Hello, John.'

'You've changed your bow again! Isn't that the same as the last time you saw me yesterday? How many times a day do you change your bow?'

Oops, I feel a little embarrassed. Now he probably thinks I'm weird for changing my bow. No, it's not the same. It is red-and-pink spots, not pink-and-red spots. They are different, I thought maybe you had worked out what it means. Nevertheless, I'm not saying anything. John, if only you could read my mind you would understand! It's for you. For how I feel about you.

'Sometimes at lunchtime I change my bow depending on how the day is going. It reflects my mood.'

There, you are the only person I have said this to. If that's not a clue, well, you can lead a horse to water, but…

'Checks to spots. You have changed from feeling square to dotty!'

At last we are communicating.

'That's close enough!'

'I've come down from my meeting. Mr Akkad is really upset the Internet has gone down and wants to know what's happening. I thought it better I come and mention it to you rather than you having to deal with him, I tell you! I told him you would deal with it, I have confidence in you, Sally.'

Confidence? What does that mean? I'm feeling nervous now.

'It's probably a supplier issue. They happen from time to time. Usually they don't last long.'

'Can I use your phone to call him?'

'Of course.'

'Mr Akkad, apparently it's a short-term problem with the service provider and should be back up soon.'

Well, well. John has a telephone business voice! I've never heard him speak like that. He sounds so formal and posh, especially in that suit. Any partner would be proud of him.

'Service provider? What's that?'

'The Internet supplier. It's a good job I shielded you from what he said!'

'Thank you.'

I am feeling nervous. Here goes, I hope this comes out right. I need to know if there is a Mrs Shedfield. Just say it nonchalantly, not giving anything away. Oh no, I can't look at him. I can't say this without looking away. I am so self-conscious, he'll notice this is a trick question!

'I like your suit, it was a surprise to see you in it.'

'I have a light suit as it's usually too hot on cruises to wear anything darker. The staff have uniforms, but I'm allowed to look a bit more like management.'

Here we go. Stare at the suit, stare at the suit, well, less of the stare!

'I am sure your wife thinks you look good in it!'

Bomb dropped. Now wait for feedback.

'Wife? No, I've never married. In this job it's too difficult, too many arguments, I've seen others try and the strain of being away so much is not worth it. It's really a younger person's job, but I've kept doing it as I've nothing to keep me onshore!'

Anything I now say will be wrong, and I'll regret it. So, what do I say?

'I hope the storm that's coming doesn't cause you problems.'

Yes, talk about the weather, you can't go wrong there!

'It shouldn't, it's not a boat, remember?'

Shut up now.

'Ha-ha.'

'OK, now I have to get back to the ship!'

No, no, you can't. I changed my ribbon. I thought you got the message.

'I hope when I get back, Sally, you'll have that drink with me!'

Yes, yes I will.

'I am not sure.'

'You have nothing to lose.'

Yes I do, my virginity!

'What?'

Oh, no. Did I think aloud? No, surely not. I'm blushing again.

'See you in two weeks!'

He better come see me when they get back. I won't be left standing on the harbour wall for the rest of my life, waiting for my sailor to return. He's gone. And I've lost my mind. What has happened to me? Have I fallen in love? It's a yucky word, tacky, not for me.

'My new flowers.'

This has been a very strange three days. Everything in my life has changed.

*

Well, if it isn't the Delaneys and the Hobarts coming to check out together. How nice! But also great, I've got to get people moving.

'Good morning! Checking out, are we?'

'Yes, Sally, it's been so nice seeing the grandchildren, hasn't it, Mary?'

'Yes, but—'

'Here's the room keys.'

Some things never change, interrupting as always! But Mary does tend to go on and on when she starts talking.

'And you, girls, how was the bed?'

'Sophie kept wriggling all night, I hardly slept.'

'No, Kylie, you were snoring! That kept waking me.'

Doubt it, I'm sure you ended up falling asleep with your phones attached to your ears, oblivious to anything!

'Sorry you weren't allowed a rollaway. But I guess you are never too old to share a bed with your sister.'

Dr Hobart is quiet. Maybe he knows better than to intervene in an argument between the girls. He can't be seen to side with one or the other, I guess!

'Dr Hobart, was everything fine with your stay?'

'Thank you, yes. Although we came down a bit early as the Internet has stopped working.'

'Yes, it is a service provider issue, it'll probably come back on soon.'

Thank you, John, for that – 'service provider' sounds so much better than 'supplier'. I really sound like I know what I am talking about! Anyway, as soon as I've checked you lot out I'll switch it back on. I need to get it running again before anyone notices it's actually turned off. I'm pushing my luck now.

'Oh, we didn't notice that, did we, Mary? Well, Sally, we must get back up the coast to our house. We don't like leaving it alone these days, you never know what might happen, even in a nice neighbourhood.'

'Grandad, you live miles from anyone else!'

'That's what makes it a nice neighbourhood!'

*

At least the lobby is noisy now and I cannot hear that awful music!

'Excuse me, is it possible to have the music turned up a bit? We have an hour to wait and it's a bit of entertainment for us.'

Entertainment? You call that entertainment? No way am I turning it up!

'I am so sorry, the volume level is set by the manager. You may be able to hear it better in the bar.'

Did I just help someone to listen to that music? What a nice girl I am!

*

'We haven't known each other long, my new flowers, but I'm going to let you into a secret. Can I trust you with it? I hope so, you are my new best friends after all.'

I am the one who turned off the Internet, it is not a service provider issue! What? Why are you looking at me so sternly? You don't approve? Surely you understand my dilemma, I had to get the cruise people down. I have never done anything like that before – well, actually I might have done if I had known how to do it. You are frowning at me again. It's harmless, and helps everybody. You don't look convinced. Hmm.

Shit, it's Mr Temple coming back into the hotel. I'd better go turn the Internet on again, he'll want to know why it's not on and the office staff will be back from their training course soon. I feel nervous. Phew, he's heading to his own office. OK, here goes, it's time for sneaky Sally! I hope there is nobody in the main office. How would I explain why I am there? Here goes. Good, the course is clear. Press the button and... lights on. The service provider has just restored the Internet! Clever Sally.

Mirror, do I look innocent or have I guilt written all over me? Is my face stuck in 'guilt mode'? No, I think I have a cheeky look, like a child who has been naughty and knows she got away with it.

*

Come on, you lot, get on the bus. You are clogging up my lobby! Dr Karlsen is talking to the Hobarts. I wonder if his kids are thinking she will make a nice girlfriend for Daddy? Maybe they would get jealous of her if he did start seeing her – kids don't always accept parents getting involved in new relationships. Well, they have a week or so at sea to find out. Please hit on him, not my John. Oops, did I say, 'my John'? Am I already getting possessive? The word that strangles relationships at birth? I hope not, especially with his job! Strange, the Hobarts are getting on the bus, but Dr Karlsen has slipped away. Why is she not getting on as well?

After all that drama over the internet, and rushing around checking everyone out, I feel exhausted. Even the bus driver looks frustrated, he's probably going to be late for the next pickup.

Here's Mr Akkad, I hope he didn't think I was looking at him. Please, please don't come here. I really don't want to check you out, especially if you are as upset as John said. Phew. He's gone to the express check-out box. He was such a strange guy. I always try to look for the good in people, but he just oozed bad. He's chatting to the bus driver, who looks agitated. I'm not surprised – if he was getting twitchy before, he will be having fits now he's facing Mr Akkad! Off goes the bus, but Mr Akkad is still there. Shit, I hope he's not coming back into the hotel. Phew, he has a driver to collect him, probably a privilege of organising the event. Either that or he doesn't want to scare the others on the bus, especially the children! I feel cold just looking at him.

*

Well, well, Alex is coming over after the rush. I wonder what for, he's walking normally this time, so obviously relaxed about this subject!

225

'Hi, Alex, I bet you are glad that lot have gone. It's been a real pain this morning, I'm exhausted.'

'You didn't have to deal with all the luggage. But that's why I am here: Dr Karlsen has forgotten her bags, she didn't collect them to put on the bus.'

I'm sure you would have noticed if she had!

'Yes, I saw the bus leave without her. She wandered off before it left, so I am not sure what's happening.'

'Maybe she's going up separately. I saw that scary guy Akkad went by private car.'

'Well, she's not checked out through me, but she could have done an express check-out, quite a lot did as the line at my desk was so long.'

'What do you think I should do?'

'Probably nothing for now, but we better send them to the boat, I mean ship, if she's not here soon. I think John, Mr Shedfield, said it doesn't leave for a few hours.'

Oops, I shouldn't have let that slip!

'John?'

Shit, don't look at me like that. I know, we never use first names for guests and senior managers. I don't want gossip.

'The guy from the cruise ship.'

'You called him John – you know him that well, do you?'

Shut up, Alex. You are such a child sometimes.

'He was here for a couple of nights and insisted I call him John. It became a habit.'

'He became a bit of a habit, did he?'

Oh, for crying out loud.

'Not that way. Go back to your bags.'

I hate that. He's going to go on and on about it every time we chat. He'll get other people to keep asking me about 'John'. This could be bad!

CHAPTER 17

CHECKING IN?

Ah, breathe out slowly. At least everything is calmer now the cruise ship people have gone.

Here come the Turners from their zoo trip. Oh dear, they have only been gone a couple of hours. I wonder what went wrong? They look like they have been arguing. Maybe over who wanted to do what at the zoo? That's normal, most families are like that, at least that was my experience as a child. But to come back so soon… the poor child, no stuffed snake for her. Maybe one of them said she couldn't have it as it's stupid. Maybe one of them didn't really want to go to the zoo and got grumpy when they were there. Maybe the girl wanted the snake and was told she couldn't have it and so an argument started, the usual sulking, and then the decision: 'If you are going to behave like that we are going home straight away', with the follow-up: 'No stuffed snake for you!' I know that one, I heard it many, many times.

'My new flowers, when I look at Mrs Turner I wonder what she feels like.'

I imagine she does everything for him that needs doing in his older age. She has her needs too, and may well feel she doesn't really ask for too much in return. He seems generous with his money, but relationships are more than that. He appears nice enough, but perhaps he's turning into a grumpy old man, and the strain is beginning to tell. She seems to ignore most of what he is saying. He doesn't need a wheelchair or mobility scooter, or anything like that yet. Not even a walking stick. The body can start to go before the mind, or vice versa. What you see on the outside may not be the same inside. What you can be certain of is one or the other will, at some stage, make life a real challenge.

*

Stay cool, Sally. Try to act normal with Mr Temple.

'Mr Temple, what can I do for you?'

'I hear the Internet went down over lunchtime?'

Shit. He's looking seriously at me. How come he's talking like it's my fault? Yes, it was, but no way can he know. It's annoying he is taking it out on me, even if I did it! Where's the *Do not abuse the staff* notice? He needs to read it. Sally, put on a happy smile.

'Yes, but it's working again now.'

'Let's hope there isn't a flood of guest comment cards or bad Internet reviews.'

'Most of the guests affected were for the cruise ship. Many left check-out until the last minute, so at least when the Internet went off they got moving.'

'Yes, housekeeping said it was a help. But it's the reputation of the hotel that's important.'

Is that all he cares about. What about the staff? Two-faced shit.

'Nobody really trusts reviews on the Internet, do they?' I like it if someone shows appreciation and mentions me. 'Anybody could write a review – competitors, ourselves even!'

'What are you suggesting?'

Shit. It's like I am challenging him. I'd better back off. Remember, Sally, you are not allowed an opinion unless asked for it first!

'Oh, nothing, I was just saying.'

'They are very important. Some people take them seriously. The hotel owners do.'

And that's what is important.

'Well, I doubt they had time to fill out comment cards, they were all in a rush to get to the bus.'

'I hope it doesn't happen again. We have a group of cricket legends arriving shortly, and they need it to keep in touch with the media.'

Why are you saying this to me? It's not my fault when the Internet goes down. Once again I have to listen to all the crap, usually due to someone else. I know full well it will go down again, guests complain about the quality of the Internet all the time. But you have to tell the boss what he wants to hear, don't you? I feel like I am telling a teacher at school that I won't do something again, promise.

'I am sure it won't, it was a service provider issue. The Internet is usually OK for a long time after it's had a problem like that. Maybe they were doing engineering work to improve the service.'

Gosh, I can talk a load of crap too!

'Where's the RDM?'

Oh no, here we go again!

'I have no idea. I guess in a meeting.'

Maybe he wants to talk to Frank about me, maybe he knows more than he's telling. Shit, I'm feeling nervous again now. I don't think I could turn the Internet off again. It's all too much stress. I will suggest it as a strategy to Frank, 'on reflection on the impact of this outage', of course. He can take the stress next time.

'Get him to call me.'

'OK, Mr Temple. I will do as soon as I see him.'

Which could be a long time.

'I see the notice isn't up yet. I hope you are not trying to hide it again!'

'No, of course not! Bill came and said he needed his ladder, so he's gone to get it.'

'OK.'

Why did he feel the need to have a dig over me removing the bloody notice? If he hadn't put it on the desk he wouldn't have had to buy a new vase of flowers! It's all his fault for not listening to me. Better chase up Bill, it's been over an hour. How long does it take to find a ladder?

'Bill, it's Sally at reception. I wondered when you are coming back? Mr Temple was just here asking.'

Might as well play the Mr Temple card up front!

'Hi, Sally, I'm out at lunch. I'm not sure where I left my ladder. But I'll be with you as soon as I get back.'

Maybe Maria didn't put it back after I saw her with it yesterday. Should I mention it? No, that might be gossiping, and I wouldn't want her to get into trouble. I feel bad about not mentioning Maria, but what can I do? Anyway, surely he has more than one ladder, maintenance is a 'department' after all! In any case, he could use a chair to stand on for this job. I do for my light bulb maintenance at home, and the notice is only going up on the wall at head height.

'Flowers, it sounded like he was in a bar.'

I hope he's capable of putting it up straight, and not falling off his ladder. He really shouldn't drink at lunchtime, not with his accident record. Oh, why did I say that? I sound like Peter! I wonder what it's like to lose your job in older age and have to take something lower than you are used to? I worry about whether, when I am older and less attractive, they will want to move me away from reception. I don't see why they should if I can do the job. I am not sure how I would cope if I had to do something else. I wouldn't want to be in the little room doing reservations. That's not as nice a job. I'd be no good in the office, I don't know how the other departments work. Did I just feel a little shiver? Yes, scary.

*

Peter's scurrying over here, I bet he saw Mr Temple leave and wants the gossip. I'm sufficiently bored that I'm actually pleased to chat for a bit.

'Hi, Sally, your espresso macchiato!'

'Thank you. It's nice and quiet this afternoon after the rush.'

'Not as quiet as you think. A lot is going on!'

Oh, really? Have you imagined it, or is something really going on?

'Do tell me, I'm not busy.'

'Well, who's this John I have heard is associated with you?'

Damn Alex, I'll kill him.

'It's nothing. I bet that was Alex, he likes to make things out of nothing.'

Especially where I am concerned! And it's not helped by you spreading gossip, you are as bad as each other.

'Has the attractive blonde left yet?'

'You mean Dr Karlsen? I assume so, she is part of the cruise group.'

'A mate of mine, Joe, saw her chatting to some guy in the bar he works at in the mall. You really cannot mistake her. He agrees, she's a real hottie!'

Probably Brandon, the guy who I think might be a private detective. I'm not feeding his gossip. A little shake-of-the-head-and-stare time.

'And?'

'Well, maybe that means something?'

'What? That she's a real hottie?'

'No, silly. Who knows what she was saying to the guy? He's a regular at the mall bar, so not part of the cruise group.'

I am not silly, you are. I am not saying anything about Brandon coming into the hotel. I am sure Peter knows nothing.

'Why do you care anyway? People who don't know each other, and have nothing going on between them, do chat in bars, you know! Maybe they were discussing the sport on the TV!'

Another Sally shake-of-the-head-and-stare.

'You're being daft again. She's far too hot to watch sport!'

'Why?'

'Well, she's a doctor isn't she?'

'And? You don't have to be dim to enjoy sport on TV!'

Although it might help. Time to roll the eyes!

'If she was a rich, intelligent hottie that loves sport, I mean, wow!'

Idiot. Time to give him one of those 'Please explain in more detail what the crap you are talking about' looks. The one that threatens to make you look really stupid if you dare to try.

'Oh, you wouldn't understand. By the way, what did the boss have to say?'

Not 'by the way' at all. This is really why he came over in the first place. You are so easy to read.

'Not much.'

'Did he mention the Internet going down?'

'Briefly.'

'It really messed up the office and reservations.'

'It was only a short service provider issue. I doubt it was as dramatic as that.'

'Thing is, I saw you do it!'

Shit. What? Did he really see me? I am in a panic, can't focus. Bugger.

'But don't worry, I won't tell anyone. You owe me for this.'

Owe him? The little shit is grinning. Like he's got me caught, trapped. Bastard. The idea he would try blackmail me is disgusting. But where did he get the idea it was me from? Nobody would guess that without some clue. He did see me hide the notice on Monday, but the lobby bar was

234

empty then, he had a clear view. But there is no way he can know this. The shit.

'You lying toad! There is no way you could have seen anything. The lobby bar was far too busy with guests.'

Sorry, toads, for saying that, don't take it personally. I hope you aren't all stupidly politically correct over things like that.

*

'My new flowers, it's so quiet!'

It sometimes gets like this: everyone has checked out, now a pause waiting for the next group to arrive. But the worse thing about it is you can hear the music! What do you think of it? It's probably new for you so nice, the guests only hear it once or twice and like it, but poor me, I have to listen to it day in and day out. You'll grow to hate it too!

*

Here comes Ed the delivery guy. Even I don't mind him breaking the monotony of this afternoon!

'Santa!'

'It's quite a contrast, here all is calm, but in the office all hell has broken out! I thought it better to leave them alone and come here.'

'Oh, what happened?'

'The Internet went down. They were all in a conference for the morning, so one of them decided to use the time to update the main computer software. They left the computer running, but when the Internet went down it stopped updating and nothing works now! They are having to redo the whole exercise, it'll take hours so they'll be late going home!'

Oh dear, what a shame, the office having to leave late. What a great shock it will be for them. They may miss the soap operas they chat about all day. I am sure they are already saying this is a tragedy worthy of any soap series. Hopefully nobody will know it was me! Maria better not say anything.

*

Well, well, well. If it isn't Dr Karlsen and that Brandon guy chatting to Alex. They are taking her bags. Come along, Alex. I want to kill you for gossiping about me, but I really want the gossip on this! Oh, yes. Look at that slow, swaggering walk, grinning like a kid with a lollipop. He knows he has something I want! No way now am I going to mention about Peter asking about John. I won't give him the satisfaction of thinking it upset me.

'I saw them, before you say anything.'

'I won't say anything then.'

Oh no, he's going to try and tease me. Idiot.

'They off to the boat, err, ship?'

'She said to tell you she used the express check-out and is now off to the cruise ship. But I don't believe them. They looked furtive.'

You wouldn't know furtive if it hit you in the face. Alex always tries to make something out of nothing. I can imagine his life is so boring he has to make up adventure stories.

'No, she'll be off to the ship, the guy is probably there to help her.'

'Not necessarily. I overheard that Akkad guy getting really pissed she wasn't on the bus.'

Big ears. Mind you, I'm as bad when it comes to fresh-but-true gossip.

'I get the impression he's always angry.'

'Well, I guess we will never know.'

I will when John comes back. And you'll never know anything about that.

*

I'd better call Maria to see how quickly they are getting through the rooms. The cricketers may start arriving soon.

'Maria, how's it going?'

'OK, but your guy Mr Akkad has trashed his room!'

'What? The suite?'

'Yes, he's made a right mess, throwing things around by the look of it. It won't be ready for the cricket boss guy for hours.'

'Mr Akkad went straight out, express check-out. If the room's trashed that's probably why. People who have messed their rooms usually avoid the embarrassment of coming to the desk! Put any extra costs for cleaning in your report and we'll bill his card.'

Well, that's Katie's problem. Just because someone's looks chill you to the bone, and you think 'gangster', you don't expect that kind of behaviour. Maybe he was on drugs or alcohol. Maybe he was just really, really pissed off. I hope he didn't fill out a guest comment card!

*

Hurrah, at last, guests to check in. Time moves so slowly when you have nothing to do. A young couple, check the fingers… yes, engaged to be married.

'Good afternoon, how can I help you?'

They are looking at each other. Come on, one of you stop letting the other go first. Someone take charge. You can't go through your whole married life coo-cooing with each other. Ah, good, the future Mrs is taking the lead.

'We have a reservation for one night, the name is—'

'Wright.'

Well, that didn't last long.

'I know, sweetie, I was just going to say that. I know that will be my married name.'

Well, sweetie, get him in order before you get married.

'Oh, how nice. When's the big day?'

'We'll be—'

'In three months.'

He's at it again! The interrupting would really piss me off.

'He's so enthusiastic. Cannot wait. We are hoping to have children too. Do you have any?'

What? Children? Imagine, a family all constantly interrupting each other. I can see them arguing over something, each cutting the other off in mid-sentence, and the volume level going up and up!

'No, not yet. I haven't found the right partner.'

'Oh, you don't need a partner, just go to the clinic and get one!'

'I'm not sure about that. The thing is, well, have you ever grown plants or taken care of a pet?'

What, did I really say that?

'No, but my father had a nice garden. We have a lovely apartment overlooking the river!'

'Don't you think you should try taking care of plants and pets before having children?'

What am I saying? I never talk to guests like this!

'Why?'

'Plants, like kids, need constant attention and patience. Pets, like kids, need constant feeding, playing with and cleaning. It's not easy, the animal rescue centre I visit is testimony to that. Surely you have to succeed with plants and animals before having children?'

Where did that come from? What am I doing?

'The building rules don't allow animals, and there is no balcony for a plant.'

'So, the children would be brought up inside? No garden to play in, no pets to care for, no fresh vegetables to grow and eat?'

Shit, have I lost self-control? What's happening? I cannot help myself. I feel like I am gushing. This is scary. I've never done this before, at least not since I was a kid.

'It's impossible, it's the best area of the city. Houses are very expensive, but there is a small park. Anyway, kids spend their lives in front of computers and the TV these days!'

That's not how I see childhood. Stop now, Sally. Stop!

'Here are your keys. Have a nice stay.'

Go away now before I lose it completely. I want to say I wouldn't trust you to bring up a hamster!

Why did I lose it? Why did I go on a rant? It's like someone has unlocked a hidden, dangerous part of me. I am always in control. The guest is always right. These people weren't nasty or aggressive, or even Mr Temple's style of abusive! Is it John, or thoughts of the little girl, Lily? Maybe my childhood – maybe the two of them have exposed some old wounds, opened me up like Pandora's box. Perhaps it's just everything coming together, a kind of personal tsunami. That's frightening. Shit! But I feel a sense of freedom. It's like a weight has been taken off me. I feel more alive.

*

'Phew, my new flowers!'

I know it's your first day, and I wanted to introduce you to my world gradually. However, today has been a hurricane of emotion. After all that excitement I feel exhausted! And now I'm bored. It's only Wednesday afternoon and so much has happened this week. In fact, it's been a very busy week on the relationship front. It started with a coffin of roses from a boring brown- suited guy, who was not at all suitable, and has all-round bad taste and lack of imagination. Meeting John has really changed things for me. I actually want to get to know him better. He is so different from my other suitors. I usually look for reasons not to date someone. Only when I cannot come up with one do I consider a date.

Obviously, Ed the delivery guy is too young and into himself. Old Mr Wood, whose wife has just died, would give me a secure pension, but I'd have to nurse him. Officer Hackness would be safe, assuming he's not married! But he's boring and probably controlling. His shirt is far too crisp and I don't want to spend my life ironing his shirts and getting into trouble because they are not just right – maybe he wouldn't even let me do them, I imagine he probably has his own way of doing everything. Mr Hill, the nervous man, he's a little older, safe, but has his personality issues. I'd have to spend my life pushing him to do things and making up for his failings, which would be very frustrating. I don't fancy him sexually, and could imagine he'd be more nervous in bed than I would be, and sex is a scary enough thought for me. Mind you, he has a daughter so is capable, assuming she is his.

I could never get involved with others at work. My job is so important, it's my life, my existence, I wouldn't want to compromise my situation. As for John himself, well, maybe I would have to be a dutiful wife and he'd play away when on cruises. But would I care, so long as it was good when he was with me?

*

Into the lobby come two older men in club blazers and shirts with club ties, white trousers and shining shoes. This surely must be the first of our cricketers. There is something about older men in blazers that looks so right, and they can even get away with wearing white trousers! It's what you should wear when you retire. Plain blue jackets are boring, blue is a cold colour, and alone it doesn't work, too much like a suit. I like stripy blazers, old private school types. But designers and schools should think about the combination of colours, both the positive and negative meanings. Changing the width of one colour relative to another is best. A pinstripe allows a bold colour's meaning to be tweaked with touch of something more sensitive. Obviously you would not want a mixed bunch of colours, that's something a comedian would wear, not at all classy!

'Good afternoon, how can I help you?'

'Hello, we are here for the cricket.'

I knew it! They are so polite – well, cricket is a posh game, isn't it? What gentlemen compared to BW. Whether they were gentlemen when younger, who knows, but now they seem happy with themselves, no need to prove anything. Retiring from any high-pressure or high-profile business must be really tough. The need to adapt to a new way of life, I can only guess how difficult that might be. Obviously some manage it better than others.

*

'My new flowers, what do you think I should wear if I go on a date with John?'

I was thinking fishnet hold-ups, with red or pink panties? You don't know this, but I have never worn fishnets. See how I am changing? I feel nervous and excited just thinking about it! But what about the bow? I always wear sheer stockings, and there are obviously spots to match hold-ups, but with fishnets, how can I get a bow that tells that story? Mind you, I guess If I wear black panties, then I can just have a simple all-black bow! Yes, but then, what goes with a black bow and fishnets? I could wear a black dress, but they can look frumpy, awful – I don't want to look like a pensioner on some Mediterranean island like I see on the TV! It's also supposed to be 'only a drink', so I guess something cocktaily is best. Maybe a tight black skirt and a pink top, not too low-cut. I want John to want to know me, not be offered it on a plate. Well, I have over a week to decide. It will be nice looking around the shops and reading magazines with a real purpose rather than as a diversion!

*

Tip-tap, *tip-tap*, hurrah! Here comes Katie!

'Hi, Sally!'

'It's been a dramatic day! The Internet went down for an hour, causing chaos. At least the cruise ship people have all left, including the scary Mr Akkad. Your cricketers have started arriving, but most have still to come.'

'What state are they in?'

'Oh, fine, these two seemed completely sober!'

'Good, not like some sports fans I could mention!'

I want to tell her about John. Especially before Alex gets to say something about it.

'I had a nice surprise today. That guy Mr Shedfield from the cruise ship came in.'

'Oh, yes, he's very charming.'

Charming? What does she mean by that? I don't want to

243

talk about him to her now. I feel the dark cloud of jealousy coming on. I wonder if he invited her out for a drink. I was so happy, and now feel like shit.

'He came in to see Mr Akkad.'

'Not you? A little bird tells me that you call him John!'

Bloody crow, more like! Alex must have caught her when she arrived and couldn't wait to say something!

'Who said that?'

'I met Bill the maintenance guy on my way in. He was looking for his ladder, and he mentioned he has to put up our notice on the wall.'

Even Katie knows he is called Bill.

'That was this morning. Look, the notice is still on the floor, leaning against the wall. He's been looking for it all day! How can you lose a ladder? It's unlikely you would forget where you left it!'

At least that's got her off the subject of John, I don't feel like telling her now. As for John, can I confide in him? Letting a human in my life after years with only the flowers, the mirror and my stuffed animals at home? John will get what he wants, and maybe, a big, big maybe, I'll get what I want too.

CHAPTER 18

TIME TO GO HOME!

'Well, my new flowers, I made it through another day. You made it through your first!'

It's disappointing that John is not around for a drink today, but it was a nice surprise to see him, and we do have a date! I have to go home now, but will be back in the morning. You won't be alone, you have Katie next, then Matt will be with you during the night.

'Goodnight, flowers, see you tomorrow at 7am!'

Once again I have homework. The hinge holding the door on a cupboard has come loose. I've fixed it before but it comes off again and again, and more frequently. I even tried gluing the screws in, with something that said it could fix anything, but the glue came off in a lump after it dried! The door will fall off if I don't fix it. So tonight on my way home I'll stop by the hardware store and ask them what to do. I wonder if John can fix a broken door? Silly girl, first of all you would never let him in your home, and second, you can do it! You do not need a man for anything! Why did I even think like that? It's so not me!

The trip to India last night with the tiger was wonderful, very colourful and musical. Tonight I am going to China with the panda. I only have tea with Chinese food. It's good to have an alcohol-free night, although very hard when a bottle is staring at you! I'll make a stir-fry with Chinese sauces. I am not sure what film to watch, there are now many new Chinese films you can get with subtitles, but I don't know anything about them. So tonight I will play it safe and watch a martial arts film. The panda likes those action films. I wonder if John has a body like that underneath his shirt. Kung fu stars don't have hairy chests and I saw a little of his poking through, I am sure he left his shirt a little more open to show it. I don't really like chest hair – like beards, they seem unhygienic, as do men with very long hair with dandruff, ugh! But at least he cares enough about himself that he hasn't let himself get a big belly. As with the smelly guy guest, a man who doesn't care about himself – well, how would I expect him to care about me?

Now, a quick check in the mirror. Yes, Sally is presentable enough for the commute home. It's 3pm and I'm out of here. Shop, take off make-up, drink, read a magazine, eat in front of the TV, bed, egg in nest, try to sleep. I'm sure I'll be fine, in fact I feel very fine indeed! It's amazing. In three days my world has changed. I will soon go on my first real adult date, and probably lose my virginity. What's best of all is I feel happy about that. I don't feel like there is anything to be really frightened of. Just happy nervousness, something to make a joke about! For the next two weeks it will be red-and-black checked ribbon days until John returns. Then, well, bring on the all-black bow!

WEDNESDAY, ABOUT 3.05PM

Sally opens the concealed door behind her desk, and passes down the corridor through the staff room. A quick glance in the mirror shows her looking tidy and she makes her way to another corridor and opens the door to the outside world. Like all staff, a nondescript side door is her exit from the stage of work.

In a buoyant mood, she feels her senses dazzled. The sun seems brighter and she squints a little. The scent of the flowers in the hotel gardens is more fragrant than ever. The birds seem to be singing louder and more joyously.

If Sally had looked, she would have seen a car moving slowly down the street. She would have noticed a rear window partly lowered. She would have recognised a familiar face. She would have seen a gun barrel.

She never knew she had been killed instantly with a single shot to the head.

Meet John, Mr Akkad, Dr Elana Karlsen, Brandon and others again in the forthcoming Galahad Porter trilogy!

For more information see:

www.galahadporter.com
Twitter: @galahadporter
Facebook: www.facebook.com/GalahadPorter
or @GalahadPorter
Email: info@galahadporter.com

AT RECEPTION:
THE JOURNEY

As I write my planned thriller trilogy, the storyline and characters are evolving. Some scenes are no longer key to the main plot. A number of hotel scenes from the novel were to be discarded. In December 2015 I stayed in several hotels and was inspired to rework the hotel scenes for separate publication. More importantly, I felt the reader should not be denied the chance to see the world through the eyes of the delightful Sally. Originally planned as a short story for e-book distribution, as the material grew a short novel became the favoured format. Eventually it evolved into a full-length novel, as chronicled in the blog on my website, which is reproduced below.

Reception staff, like others employed in dealing directly with the public, may seem to be machines processing people. But for the person involved it's a tortuous, schizophrenic world of saying one thing and thinking another. Losing the plot with a guest is not allowed.

Did you care about Sally by the end of the novel? Probably not. People are usually more comfortable not knowing what people, including friends, really think.

The decision to include Sally's death in *At Reception* was

controversial. It was suggested to me that the book is about Sally's life at reception, so her death is unnecessary and it's a mistake to include it. It would have been easy to leave out the last two sentences. However, her shooting is a key nexus in the thriller that ties various characters and plots together. I felt to ignore it would be deceptive. The reader, if hoping for romance between Sally and John, would buy Part 1 of the trilogy only to find out she dies in the next paragraph.

You may wonder who shot Sally. There are several candidates, but you, the reader, have only Sally's perspective on the people she has met. Do not assume someone who appears in front of her is as nice as they seem. The identity of the assassin may come out in the trilogy, but not knowing who shot Sally keeps the suspense over which character is capable of murder. Maybe, as the trilogy evolves, her death will become as insignificant as her life. A sad reflection on society.

Galahad Porter, January 2017.

THE BLOG

The blog below chronicles my experience while writing *At Reception*. I have formatted it as a diary, allowing the reader to understand some of the issues a new writer has to deal with from the time they start tapping at the keyboard to publication. I have also added a few retrospective comments to the entries to add more depth to the subjects covered.

This is as up-to-date as the book publication timetable allowed, so for subsequent blogs see the website, Facebook and Twitter. There are photos associated with many of these articles, which are not reproduced here but can be found on my website at www.galahadporter.com/the-blog.

14th November 2015

How Fast Do I Write?

I tend to write 1,000 words in a typical day, with 2,500 words maximum. Writing a book is not just about typing – there is research to do, and corrections, changing characters, timelines and subplots… oh, and dealing with the website, social media etc.! And that's before we even get to marketing, agents, publishers, conferences etc.! I average about 5,000 words a week. So for 125,000 for a book = twenty-five weeks minimum. However, I am writing a trilogy, so some of my writing is for Books 2 and 3. If you see my website (www. galahadporter.com), you will see I suggest that the draft of Part 1 should be ready by Q3 2016, and the other two in mid 2017.

Note: Oh, what optimism I had when I embarked on the journey! The simple maths of dividing word count total by words typed per week proved irrelevant. What I had not realised was how much time would be spent redrafting so-called 'final versions'. I currently expect all three books to be ready by late 2018.

21st November 2015

Have I Any Problems With 'Writer's Block'?

Not at all, although it can happen to a writer at any time! At the moment I have the opposite problem, when ideas flow faster than I can write. I am a compulsive list-writer. I get ideas all the time. I wake at 1am and get up and scribble things down, otherwise I can't get back to sleep. I keep a notebook around 24/7 in case I get an inspiration – I noticed a woman behave in a particular way at Heathrow Airport and *had* to write it down before I forgot it!

At the start of a writing session I transfer my latest notes to the laptop. That way I can edit/expand/cut and paste the idea into the novel. I find that helps get me 'in the zone' and ready to write. I sometimes plan to write a particular scene I have been thinking about, but suddenly a burst of inspiration sends me off elsewhere! My most inspired work is when the floodgates open – fortunately there are spelling and grammar checkers for afterwards! Let's hope the flow continues!

29th November 2015

What Would You Call Your Dog in Japanese?

Choosing names and sexes is a challenge! Characters (and pets) have to have a name, cultural background, personality, opinions, physical characteristics, age, employment status, sex and sexual orientation etc.

I find naming the characters particularly difficult, as any parent will know when it comes to naming their own children! You try avoid choosing names for characters that are similar to real people. For a lead character I used an anagram of a name. Really obscure, you would think? Not the case! On searching the Internet it was the actual name of a Spanish person who worked in the same profession!

Naming people born in different years and different countries/cultures is tough. Some names go out of fashion, or are modern and were not used at that time. So you have to search for names popular in that year, e.g. Dutch baby boy first names in 1970.

For non-English names you need to know the meaning of the translation, just in case it's inappropriate for the character! A Japanese girl called Makoto, which means 'sincerity' in English, may not be a good name for a murderess... depending on your sense of humor!

If you think human names are hard, choosing a dog's name in Japanese *and* deciding which sex it should be took ages! Fortunately there are lists of popular Japanese female dog names... but I still haven't chosen the breed!

5th December 2015

Fatigue Can Be Physical and Mental

I have no shortage of what I think are great ideas; imagination is not a problem. Some might say my imagination *is* my problem!! But after writing for a long period (say, over two hours), I feel mentally somewhat drained and a little tired. It's like part of your brain has been downloaded onto the computer! I think I put a lot into my work and don't realise because I enjoy it so much! It's best to try to limit yourself, but when in full flow...

Physically you cannot write long sections on a laptop – scrolling the small screen drives you nuts and is bad for posture, eyesight and the risk of repetitive strain injury (RSI). You need a big, and preferably multiple screens – I plug my laptop into a monitor, and use a wireless keyboard and mouse. I also need space around me for bits of stuff, and scribbling – yes, paper still exists in the writer's world! I don't yet have a touchscreen monitor, but am coming to the conclusion that it would be a good idea. At least I would get the exercise of lifting my hands above keyboard level occasionally… except I tend to dip into a bowl of red hot chilli puff snacks when writing and wiping the screen regularly would be a pain!

16th December 2015

Sex

I've never understood why authors feel obliged to include sex scenes. 'Written sex' is boring to me, has never really turned me on, and I feel like I am reading a sex manual! A photo has a lot more impact. Adding sex scenes with no significant bearing on the plot irritates me. There is nothing worse than having to sit through sex scenes in films that seem overly extended relative to other scenes, or possibly included at the expense of another, more interesting storyline! I am told a writer should cut out everything that is not vital to the plot…

For sex to be good in a book you have to get inside the minds of the participants, and see it from the characters' differing perspectives. Writing sex scenes is pointless unless sex in a relationship is a key story in itself.

At the moment I have no descriptive sex scenes – I am hoping the sexual tension between characters will be rewarding enough for those of you who need it!

Do I sound like a prude? I have been doing research; there is plenty of advice out there on the Internet. If you think you can convince me of a particular way to portray sex when written, let me know at info@galahadporter.com, and you may get a treat somewhere in the trilogy!

2nd January 2016

Any Reputation Is Better than No Reputation!

I was told a long time ago that any publicity, good or bad, is better than no publicity at all! For the writer, 'reputation' is important. Is it better to have any reputation, good or bad, than no reputation at all?

A writer's public reputation starts with their first published work, e.g. journalism, a short story or an article. The track record provides a publisher with a guide as to what to expect. What about the unpublished writer with no reputation and first manuscript ready? For a publisher, to take on a first novel and put effort into promoting the writer (not just the book) can be difficult to justify.

Modern self-publishing companies allow an unknown writer to get into print and start to build a reputation. However, self-publishing your first novel, containing all the big ideas that drove you to write in the first place, is not the approach I plan to take. If you really want to see your novel in airport bookshops around the world you need a mainstream publisher. I have a message and I want it read and, hopefully in film, heard! But I have no reputation…

As I write the trilogy the storylines and characters are evolving. Some of my earlier writing is no longer key to the main plot. I am thinking of reworking one of the scenes, and self-publishing this as a short story in paperback and e-reader formats.

Maybe it's the time for Galahad Porter to get a reputation, any reputation…!

9th January 2016

The Joy (or Not) of Working Outside!

Imagine the writer sat with their laptop in the shade of an umbrella or palm tree, by a swimming pool or tranquil sea, typing away. Improve the image with a colourful fruit-encrusted cocktail, with its own little umbrella, by the keyboard. Been there, tried it, and love it!

Alas, it's usually more fantasy than reality. Usually the glare of the sun would make writing difficult, your own reflection staring back at you behind the page! Then the risk of wind blowing any papers into the pool must not be underestimated. I end up pinning things down with anything I can lay my hands on. The mobile phone holds down something from the breeze, only for everything to fly away on instinctively picking up the phone in response to the ping of a message! I now use a cat's meow as the ringtone. It usually makes me look around for a cat before picking it up, so that gives me a second to save the paperwork!

I am an avid bird feeder – feeding seagulls in Weymouth, England, nearly got me in trouble with the authorities in the past! I keep the garden bird feeder in Australia full of fruit and sunflower seeds, which attract a wide variety of wild birds, especially rainbow lorikeets. The problem with working outdoors in such a setting is that the laptop provides a lovely perch, the keyboard a playground.

Refilling my glass indoors and returning to find a bird perched on the laptop, or typing a secret message, is a regular event. Then there is the risk of poo…

Nevertheless, an outdoor job is nice... I wanted to be a refuse (trash) collector when I was young, but I guess a writer is next best thing!

16th January 2016

How's Your Handwriting?

Inspired by a possible scene for the book, I got up at 1am. I could not be bothered to turn on the computer so started writing with a pen and paper. My first words were almost 2cm tall, and realised I needed to write a bit smaller. I was writing as fast as possible so I didn't forget any of my ideas. After the first few sentences I realised my writing would be illegible in the morning, so had to write the letters more carefully. I then got stuck guessing how to spell a word, resulting in three versions of it. I then wanted to change a sentence but there was no space unless I wrote in very tiny writing. At the end of the first page my hand was struck by cramp!

The next morning I looked at what I had written. It was a mess – rather than cramp, a teacher's ruler would have struck my hand at school!

When much younger I applied for a job and the company asked for a sample of my handwriting to send to a graphologist (see www.britishgraphology.org). The interviewer was so impressed at the results they offered me the job (I hope for other reasons too). In those days my writing was neat and tidy, looked very logical. Today a spider would feel insulted! My notebook is full of scrawl, some of which I struggle to read. I wonder what the graphologist would make of it now! Maybe, Creative Writer, would be the analysis?

23rd January 2016

The Woman You See!

I have a character. She's a Scandinavian woman. Think about her.

She works in a hospital. Think about her again.

If I mention she is a medical researcher, hold that image in your mind.

How would she prepare to have sex?

Did you say, 'She takes off her glasses and lets down her hair?'

But I never said she had glasses, nor that her hair was tied up!

If, halfway through a novel you are reading, your medical researcher buys and reads enthusiastically a celebrity gossip magazine, what would your reaction be?

Did you say, 'No way! She would never do that!'?

You become uncomfortable with the book, you have lost your feel for your character and link to the story. You may even stop reading it in disgust! It's the same thing with seeing the film adaption of a book. Isn't it awful when the characters are not as you imagined them?

But why wouldn't a medical researcher want to read celebrity gossip? If I want her to, then I have to build up to it so it isn't a shock, it's a pleasant surprise for the reader! It's not just about writing characters you can see in your own mind, it's also getting a feel for how the reader will visualise and relate to them. I hope the above demonstrates how the writer and reader can have very different perspectives on what characters are like – and that can make writing very difficult!

7th February 2016

Update on Short Novel

At the beginning of January Galahad Porter mentioned in his blog that he was considering reworking some deleted scenes from the trilogy he is writing, and publishing them as a short story. Today he is pleased to announce that he has almost reached the target of twenty-five thousand words, and by the end of February it should be suitable for copy-editing. It is planned to release an approximately seventy-five-page paperback novel, and make it available in some e-reader formats.

He has chosen the first-person style of writing, where everything is from the perspective of the main character, who is a woman. It is less popular than the more common third-person writing, but produces great dramatic effect. You are there, living inside her head, with all her thoughts and emotions. More on this subject is available in today's blog.

The trilogy continues to progress, a little slower than planned. He continues to add great new ideas to the storylines for all three parts! The first draft of Part 1 is still on schedule to be completed by the end of Q3 this year.

Note: This was written as a media release, hence the style. Once again, my forecasting is dreadful, but more on this later.

7th February 2016

First-Person Issues for the Short Novel

I blogged at the beginning of the year that I am considering publishing a short novel, based on some deleted scenes from the trilogy I am writing. As mentioned in the latest newsletter, this project has moved ahead and a first draft should be ready for editing by the end of February.

I have chosen the first-person style of writing, where everything is from the perspective of the main character, who is a woman. It is less popular than the more common third-person writing, but produces great dramatic effect. You are there, living inside her head, with all her thoughts and emotions.

There are many challenges in approaching a story with this technique. In a sense, everyone who has ever written in this style is writing about the same person, a human. Humans have many things in common, although each has a unique combination of personality and physical traits. The interaction of the character with differing situations makes such stories interesting.

Obviously, it is impossible not to have some elements of your character that are similar to those in other works. Many conversations are pretty standard, e.g. 'Good morning, how can I help?' and specific actions and emotions/humour are typically human, e.g. checking one's hair in a mirror and thinking about it.

The challenge is avoiding basing a character on yourself. It's sometimes hard to detach your own opinions from those of the character. It is necessary to get into the head of the character, and try to bring out a compelling story from what can be largely mundane actions and situations.

How far you go with psychology is a difficult call, the character needs depth without overdoing it.

I hope the reader will identify with her thoughts and feelings, and see her as a friend who is struggling to cope. More on all this soon!

13th February 2016

How I Write Is Changing!

As the short novel and trilogy progress, the way I write is changing. I used to sit at the screen and type anything that came into my head, watching the word count rapidly grow. Now, as the words become a novel, the pieces need assembling, editing and turning into something approaching the final format. Ideas have to become actions and conversations, locations need describing etc. The word count growth seems to crawl along, a thousand words adds 1% now, not the 10% or so of early days. It feels like one step backwards for two steps forward – deleting a paragraph, then replacing it with two paragraphs closer to, but still likely to be a long way from, the final version!

Most of my writing is now done between 11am

and 2pm, usually turning ideas from previous days, and sometimes months, into actual text for the novel. Outside of this period, ideas come to me and get noted for future use.

When I started writing, ideas would open new storylines and the words flowed. Now any change has to be integrated into the existing framework. I expect this to become a real pain. For an organised person having to reorganise whole storylines is very annoying, but it's necessary to keep improving!

You may think writing seems like a jigsaw, putting the various plot pieces together. But it's *much* more difficult! The pieces have to be assembled in space and time. Each piece is flexible, it can be bent, twisted, shrunk and stretched – it is not always easy to tell what goes where! You sometimes feel lazy, the challenge is too much to take on, and want to leave some pieces out – but who wants a book full of holes?!

To work on the jigsaw I find I need to keep printing sections out, and then occasionally the whole thing. It is then laid out in front of me: initially it fitted on the dining table, and now it's on the floor, and eventually will be any surface I can find! I need this to help me both see and *feel* the balance between sections, and look for obvious bits that have not been rewritten. You cannot do this on a screen, not even over two monitors. Recently I discovered I had not written any conversation for a character, although he was busy doing things! The use of ink, paper, the shredder and the recycling bin is rising!

The one thing I am not yet sure about is how much of the book I will be able to remember! I don't want to have to keep rereading the whole thing to find the odd paragraph that needs linking with something else! I am sure I'll be revisiting this subject again during the later stages of rewriting!

17th February 2016

Promotional Campaigns

There will be a number of trials of Galahad Porter promotional materials ahead of the short novel launch. A trial is planned for February 19th–March 4th in Brisbane, London and Singapore. Other locations are still to be decided. If you see any Galahad Porter publicity please let me know via info@galahadporter.com.

If you would like Galahad Porter promotional products an online shop is planned to open to coincide with the launch of the short novel.

Note: I found using a combination of drink coasters, bookmarks and printed galahadporter.com T-shirts worked reasonably well. They generated website hits, and a few extra followers on social media. But the overall impact was less than expected. One of the problems is that the book title, *At Reception*, was only a provisional working title until the publisher had been agreed. As a consequence, any publicity related purely to Galahad Porter, and I am sure you agree novels are more interesting than writers! By the time you read this an *At Reception* campaign should be well underway – see my blog for details about how that has gone.

21st February 2016

Office and SoA

Ahead of the planned short novel publication the Galahad Porter office service has been established in London. The details are:

Office address:
Galahad Porter
18 Soho Square
London
W1D 3QL
United Kingdom
Telephone: UK: 0203 790 9276
Int: +44 203 790 9276

Note that I do not write at this address, the office is for trade and marketing purposes.

I am pleased to announce that I have been accepted as a member of the Society of Authors, see their website www.societyofauthors.org for details.

5th March 2016

Update on the Short Novel – *At Reception*

I have provisionally titled the short novel *At Reception*, as it deals with events in the lobby of a hotel.

As the storyline evolved it became a deeper and more

psychological novel than originally planned. This has required extensive rethinking of the scenes, especially as it is written in first person. I now expect to finish the current draft in late March. The draft will be sent to an editor to correct errors in grammar etc. I then have to tweak it prior to submission to agents and publishers, and in parallel prepare for self-publishing as a paperback and e-book. The novel is unlikely to be accepted by a mainstream publisher as it is shorter than their usual requirements. However, I feel I must give the book a chance to sell itself, based on the size of its target market.

A little prematurely, but so I can start a debate on the issues raised in the book, the following have been set up:

Twitter: @atreception
Facebook: At Reception
www.galahadporter.com/at-reception
Please like/follow me on the above and when a critical mass has been achieved I'll kick things off!

Note: Separate accounts for each book is probably a good idea, but my experience is that everyone is happy to follow Galahad Porter, so I am not sure they are needed. Time will tell.

10th March 2016

London Book Fair

I'll be taking a short break from finishing *At Reception* to attend the London Book Fair, which runs April 12th–14th. It's pretty obvious why I am there: everybody who is anybody should be there! I won't be describing every nuance as I don't have social media activated on my mobile. I have never needed to go before, so will blog my experience as a novice after the event! See http://www.londonbookfair.co.uk for details.

10th March 2016

Do You Get Told You Are Wasting Your Life Away?

One lesson I have learned in life is that nothing you do is ever a waste of time! At least not if you become a creative writer!

I read somewhere that the best writers are older as they have more 'life experience' to draw on. Well, it's not just age, it's what you have done in that time. Spending your working life in the same job is not the same as backpacking and partying all over the world in your youth. You can still be young and have a lot more 'life experience' than someone else.

I remember learning to scuba-dive in the Caribbean in the middle of the week. I had given up full-time work a year earlier, and my ex-colleagues would have been working that week. They probably thought, *What a waste!*

Not at all – I have accumulated a rich seam of experience to mine. Well, except those times that were so colourful I never managed to recall them the next day! Of course it is possible to write a good yarn synthetically. A little research, imagination and visualisation of scenes are a basis. But truly original ideas need a good dash of experience to make them come alive.

Don't let anyone call you a waster – you never know when you might need your waste of time!

Note: The photo with this blog shows rainbow lorikeets in my garden. They watch me write and chatter between themselves… I wonder what they say. 'Waster, waster, waster!'

9th April 2016

Baubles and All That

The short novel, provisionally titled *At Reception*, is undergoing its third rewrite! Based on deleted scenes from the thriller trilogy, it is written in the first person and set in a hotel lobby. There is one more rewrite to go, then I should be close to having it ready.

The original idea was to put out a short novel to just 'get a reputation'. However, the first draft looked a little dull, like a Christmas tree with no decorations. It had structure but no personality. I decided the main character needed more depth. The result was that our tree got lights, but they glowed dimly, and seemed disconnected! The storylines needed weaving together, so the tree is currently getting strands of tinsel. I still feel it needs a few baubles to really bring it to life! Hence the need for another rewrite. The manuscript should be ready by the end of May.

The trilogy continues to progress, albeit slowly. Some substantial new ideas will mean that once the short novel is finished there will be no shortage of material to work on!

Note: By this stage the trilogy was gathering cobwebs. The expansion of *At Reception* was taking up all my time. However, your mind never totally switches off, and I continue to have some great ideas that I type up in summary form for use later.

9th April 2016

Which Publication Route?

A visit to a bookstore will confirm that very few short novels (novellas) get on the main fiction shelves, and those you find are usually by established authors. I had planned to forget going via the agent/major publisher route, as that would be unlikely to be successful, and delay publication even further.

However, two things have conspired to encourage me to at least give it a go.

Firstly, as a consequence of repeated rewriting the manuscript is getting longer. Secondly, timing. There are two book launch periods for a new writer to avoid. The first is the spring sell-in to bookstores for the summer holiday reading season. I'd be competing with bestseller authors and have no chance. The other is the autumn sell-in to bookstores for the winter holiday period, where biographies of celebrities and cookbooks abound.

If I want the short novel in bookstores I need to give

about six months' notice. The book industry works that way. If I don't want my little Christmas tree left in a corner lost amongst the big shiny celebrity trees I should wait until early 2017 to launch. This buys me a couple of months to test out a few smaller publishers and selected agents.

The style of the short novel is not representative of the main trilogy, although the central characters do overlap. If an agent/publisher loves the book and it does well they will want something else in the same style.

All in all, working with a serious, full service self-publisher is probably the best route. I can then get on with finishing the trilogy, and go the traditional agent route with that. The London Book Fair should make clear the best road to take.

30th April 2016

The London Book Fair and the Road Ahead

I am back writing after the London Book Fair. I did get a real insight into how the book industry works, and recommend any budding book writer of any genre to experience it. It allows a peek behind normally closed office doors to see what book publishing is all about. I am now much clearer about the road ahead for both the short novel and the trilogy.

In the latest newsletter and blog I said that the short novel was 'falling between the two stools' of mainstream publishers and self-publishing. It is too good a story not to give agents a chance to assess it for marketing to the bigger publishers, but at the same time too short a novel for it to have a chance of being accepted. After the London Book Fair, it is quite clear that I need to take the story from novella to novel size if I want any chance of getting it onto bookstore shelves.

The story currently covers a period of two days. Fortunately, the third day is already written as part of the main trilogy. So by taking the third day as a basis, converting it to first-person writing, I can add 50% to the book. This will have the effect of adding over fifteen thousand words to the word count. Considering the original plan was for around twenty-five thousand words, I now have a new word count target of sixty thousand words, which translates to a book of over two hundred pages, just long enough. I could still find agents or publishers demanding a bit more, but at least there is enough to run with for now.

I will update you again on progress once I have finished writing, which should be before the end of May.

Note: This blog had a photo of a lorikeet perched on my laptop, with a couple of its friends looking on. The caption: *Hey, guys! Waster is back writing! No sign of a manuscript though... nope, not here... no, not down there... no, not behind here...*

21st May 2016

Homage to Lists!

I love lists, and, oh, spreadsheets, they take them to the next dimension!

It has been suggested I have some element of obsessive-compulsive disorder (OCD) as my list-writing is extensive. But I find they bring order to my life, and at least I don't forget people's birthdays or items when shopping, well, unless they are not on the list!

For the writer, lists and their close allies the spreadsheets are really useful. When you get an idea for a book the first thing you do is start writing. Some people just keep writing to the end. Others, like myself, set up story timeline sheets and character lists. For each book I have a spreadsheet listing characters down the left, and chapter numbers/times across the top, to ensure everything happens in the correct sequence. It shows where in the book a character does something, reducing rereading to track down the odd paragraph! It also stops you leaving a loose end, for example if someone travels somewhere and you forget they have to travel back at some stage – losing a character is not allowed!

The trilogy novels have months as time units. An important character is pregnant, so I have to make sure things happen at the correct stage of her pregnancy. Whilst some will disagree, I would be pushing the credibility of my character if at nine months she is climbing mountains and trekking across the desert! I do need her to give birth, and at the correct time!

The short novel, provisionally titled *At Reception*, originally covered two working days in a hotel lobby. The timeline spreadsheet was a big help when I decided to add a third day, turning the novella into a novel. I use one-hour periods so the characters' comings and goings are kept in sequence. The spreadsheet helped with reworking the storylines. Some characters would stay an extra night, linking the days together, and consequently their stories have become more rounded and deeper. I could see where routine activities needed to fit in, the importance of which will become apparent when you read the novel. I've reproduced below a copy of the timeline sheet with the original notation for the addition of the third day.

Discipline is crucial when using lists and spreadsheets. You must not get lazy about updating. Most importantly, your writing should never become a prisoner to the sheets. Let the story come to you, don't let your initial ideas stop you from developing in a completely different direction. Having the timeline sheet on a computer helps as you can move things around easily. Nevertheless, the temptation not to change things is great, it's a lot of work and a real pain! However, the rewards in quality are worth it. When you read the final result you find it hard to believe you were once satisfied with the original version!

21st May 2016

Who Will You Party With?

I am pleased to announce that I have now got through the fifty thousand-word barrier for the novel provisionally titled *At Reception*! There are still some sections that need rewriting and, with the deepening of the storylines, the target of sixty thousand words should be met. After that it will only require checking and tweaking. During June a final version should be complete, and sent to a few selected agents to assess. It will also go for copy-editing in preparation for self-publishing, should that be needed. Release is still planned for early 2017.

I'll permanently leave Australia to return to the UK in July for meetings, and get on with the thriller trilogy until the marketing of *At Reception* starts. An update will be given at the end of June in the next edition of the newsletter.

Note: Relocating to the UK was much more distracting than expected. But, worse, each time I reread a new draft there were significant revisions on almost every page. Typing these up took as long as reviewing, and the turnaround for each draft was measured in weeks.

4th June 2016

Dealing with Psychological Issues Unsupported and Untreated

The lead character in the short novel, provisionally titled *At Reception*, struggles to cope with her life. Don't we all?

Finding your own way to deal with challenges that arise in your life is normally the first step. Failure to manage the issues usually means the need for help and support. If you get support maybe you can stop things getting worse. For example, someone who feels depressed could go to the doctor. By requesting psychiatric help before the doctor prescribes an anti-depressant, maybe it will be possible to find a way of dealing with problems and avoid taking the drugs.

But where a person does not seek support, for whatever reason, dealing alone with personal issues can be physically and mentally exhausting.

I like the idea, as in autism, of a spectrum, a range of degree of any attribute. To have a fear of water is one thing, to be truly terrified by it is different in degree. I prefer not to pigeonhole people into one condition, but see people as living on a matrix of spectra. When I look at myself I could think of several 'conditions' I may have, e.g. OCD due to my love of lists. My dislike of having my routines changed by others could be Asperger's. My great sadness that my football team were for years (and remain) demoted from the big time could be depression. Put that lot together and… you get another human being!

Each of us handles personal challenges in different ways and with varying degrees of success. I started using lists and diaries as a way of not forgetting. My tropical fish never get fed twice, probably to their annoyance!

In *At Reception*, which is written in the first person, the lead character lives alone and works largely isolated from her colleagues, but surrounded by people. You see, from her perspective, how she handles the challenges in her life and work in her own way, untreated and unsupported. I hope readers will feel a great empathy for her, identify with some of her issues and methods of dealing with them, and see her as a friend struggling to cope.

19th June 2016

Boring, Boring Galahad!

I wish I had started writing fiction years ago.

In 2005 I left my tropical life in Miami, and its sports

bars, to concentrate on living in my house in the hills of Umbria, Italy. Unfortunately I never found a partner to share the isolation of a hilltop farm, so I filled my days with sport on TV. But not just daytime. I would get up in the early hours to watch Miami Heat play basketball, or the Miami Dolphins playing American football.

If only I had used those hours writing, how much further along I would be!

I sold the Italian house and spent more time in the UK and Brisbane, Australia. I anticipated spending time watching sport. But the writing has taken over. I wake in the middle of the night thinking about the book, not whether I want to get up and watch a football game.

I am told by some friends that I have become boring as all I talk about is the progress of the book. Like a parent who constantly tells you about their child's progress, it's nice to know, but not too much of it! At least I don't have a photo album to show you! By the way, my photos of birds are more popular on Facebook than what I write! Maybe I should become a photographer…

Hopefully after the first publication I'll get a better balance. At least from next month I'll be in the UK full-time, so European and a lot of global sport will be on TV at a reasonable time of the day!

Oh, and, just to be boring, the novel provisionally titled *At Reception* is in its late rewrite stage, no major changes planned, and it shouldn't be more than a few weeks before it is ready to go! I can then bore people with the progress of the thriller trilogy! That could end up as five books if I add a prequel and Part 4. The prequel would answer the question

'I don't understand what the first three books were about'! Part 4 is my wishful thinking, it is designed to set the stage for a TV series based on some of the core characters! All this could keep me from watching sport for a few more years!

Are you asleep yet?

For the uninitiated, *Boring, Boring* is a UK football chant…

Note: Revealing the expansion of the trilogy shows that I had not stopped thinking about it. When you write a novel you have a starting date and time. But your characters had a life before that. You must know your characters' history before they appear in your novel; it defines them when they first appear. I had a particularly inspirational idea for the former lives of some of the trilogy characters, which I'd love to share as a prequel. But you will have to wait until after Part 3 is published. One advantage with writing fiction is you can change history to suit your story. So until Part 3 is finished, time can change!

25th June 2016

Forecasting: Stockbroking vs. Laundry vs. Writing

A crash outside at 2am wakes me up. My mind turns to the laundry left hanging out overnight, soaking wet as the weather forecast was wrong, again. *Is that the possum on the line, getting its messy paws all over my clothes? Forget it and go back to sleep, you can always wash them again tomorrow.*

Are you of the generation that thinks drying clothes involves only a tumble dryer? People used to put their laundry outside to dry. In reality in the UK, 'drying' outdoors frequently consists of turning something wet into something damp. My mum describes the process as being 'to lighten', reducing the water content before putting it 'to air' or on a heated radiator, or into the tumble dryer.

In Australia I have a combination washing machine/ dryer. The great disappointment at the so-called drying cycle means I hang clothes outside. Ah, you think, how lovely, a tropical environment, your clothes must smell like a bottle of fabric conditioner! Alas, this is not true. My things smell of mould. Tropical life involves a lot of trees and humidity and mouldy smells! Oh, and possum paw-prints and pee, with lashings of parrot poo.

When I worked in investment banking I used to make forecasts of company profits. When companies announce their results the markets react to whether they were better or worse than stockbroker expectations. Whilst there was some kudos for the individual in forecasting the exact result, getting it wrong with everyone else was no big deal.

Forecasting weather for drying laundry is a far more serious business! Getting it wrong can have dire consequences, especially in tropical environments where a clear, sunny sky can cloud over at any time and rain! The Internet has enabled the nerd in me to flourish in the field of laundry meteorology! I look at weather.com and the local weather bureau websites and combine their forecasts. But what does a 30% or 70% chance of rain really mean? The stars of laundry planning are the Doppler radar screens. You can see exactly where rain is coming from, pretty well live, and plan your hanging programme between bands of rain or storm cells. Exciting, eh? I don't know anyone else who does this, but I do recommend the effort!

So why am I telling you this, you wonder? Because boring, boring Galahad (see previous blog) has to say that the above are nothing compared to the difficulty of forecasting when a manuscript will be ready! Here is a sample of my forecasts for the novel provisionally titled *At Reception*:

7th February 2016: *a first draft should be ready for editing by the end of February.*

5th March 2016: *I now expect to finish the current draft in late March.*

30th April 2016: *Once I have finished writing, which should be before the end of May.*

27th May 2016: *During June a final version should be complete.*

19th June 2016: *It shouldn't be more than a few weeks before it is ready to go.*

At the time I really believed each estimate was possible. However, something always came up and changed the goalposts, adding a deeper psychological basis, producing a novel rather than a novella.

I read a couple of books on how to write novels. Whilst they were interesting in theory, and I have taken on board some of their key principles, the finer points of writing had to be largely ignored. In practice, if I had followed all their advice I would probably never finish writing! However, both were right to say it will take longer to complete a manuscript than you think, and you need plenty of time to keep improving it once you get to your word count goal.

When it comes to the forecasts for the thriller trilogy, I hope you treat them with the respect they deserve…

22nd August 2016

You will be pleased to know I have finished relocating back to the UK and it's time to get the ball rolling again on the publication of the novel provisionally titled *At Reception*, and writing the thriller trilogy!

For those not familiar with the publishing industry, here is how the process of publishing *At Reception* should go. For those who are aware of it I suggest scrolling down to the cute photo of lorikeets beating a path to my door… as I hope agents, publishers, media and anyone else who wants to know or have a slice of me will!

Those of you who have followed the saga of *At Reception* will be aware that originally it was planned to be a short novel (novella). It was to be self-published (i.e. at my expense) this year to showcase my writing, and get a reputation as a writer, no matter what kind of reputation! Based on characters from the trilogy, it was seen as a promotional item to open the doors of major agents and publishers, which are largely closed to unpublished writers.

The strategy changed earlier this year. The book evolved into a deeper, more psychological story, and later I took the view that it deserved the chance to get a mainstream publisher, and become available to a wider audience. To achieve this it was necessary to double the word count, as novellas rarely make it to UK bookstore shelves.

Major UK publishers do not accept direct submissions

from authors. First the writer has to be accepted by a literary agent. The agent usually requires a synopsis of the story, plus the opening chapters. If they like the work, which can take a couple of months to find out, they will request a copy of the whole novel. If they like that they may take you on. Agents know their clients and may require rewriting of the novel to make it more marketable. If the agent finds a publisher, the publisher may also require further modification, to meet what it sees as the marketplace, and bookstore demands. Needless to say, all this delays eventual publication, but, if accepted, the wait is worth it.

However, only a very small percentage of unpublished writers will get a major agent or publisher. Therefore, in parallel to the agent route, I will kick off the process for self-publishing, targeting launch in early 2017. The process for this starts with copy-editing. After incorporating changes and corrections it will go for typesetting. The book industry works on around six months' notice of a new title, so the publication details will be issued ASAP after I sign with the self-publisher. I'll give an update on this in a few weeks once I have an agreement.

Note: See the website blog for the photo.

12th November 2016

Going Round and Round in Circles!

How many times do you read the same book? Once? Maybe twice after a year or two? Not only did I write the manuscript for the book provisionally titled *At Reception*, I now have to repeatedly reread it, note the errors and make changes that improve it, and then type it all up again. Then I have to repeat that cycle all over again and again. If you find the novel boring the first time, imagine how I might feel? Fortunately I like the storyline and am absorbed into the events and characters. They come alive in my keystrokes, and for me it's a delight.

But I am under immense self-inflicted time pressure. The manuscript should have been off to agents and my self-publisher a month ago and, I own up, it isn't. Once again, as with every stage of the book writing process, I am finding everything takes much longer than expected. Hopefully it will be ready by the end of November.

Do you recall when you wrote your first short stories for English classes at school? The ones that were no more than a page or two of handwriting? Every sentence had to be carefully constructed. You could only rub pencil out one or two times, and rewriting the whole thing would delay watching TV. By the time you got to the end of the page you knew you had finished. This was reinforced by submission deadlines that were immovable, and there were dire consequences if the work was not given in on time!

Using a computer you type away, riding a torrent of ideas. You rack up thousands of words of text with no thought of submitting it to anyone any time soon, and definitely not at school tomorrow. The words flow onto your screen in a raging stream. You even panic when you have too many ideas at once and fear you will forget one whilst still typing up previous inspirations.

In the world of fiction you are left with a novel, yes, but it's really only a mass of words that, if you don't edit correctly, could turn into a literary compost heap.

I worked for a number of banks in the City of London. I would read investment documents to check the spelling etc. Every word was important, some people may invest a lot of money based on your exact phrasing. As a consequence my editing reading speed is slow. How fast do you read? For me it's around thirty typical novel pages an hour. That may seem slow to some, but I've always tried to pick up the nuances, the secret lines between the lines. After all, the writer has spent time stressing and thinking about every word in every sentence, so why should I just skip over them?

At Reception is not a light novel. Like many writers' first novels it's concentrated and intense. If you try to read it quickly you will miss many of the key points. As it's written in the first person, it should be read as if you are there, in conversation with a friend. A sip of coffee or wine between every paragraph. Take it in, absorb the ideas and build your relationship with the lead character.

I suffered as a teenager for making that kind of comment! When I was a schoolkid one English teacher set an exercise asking the class to each write a poem and bring it to the next lesson. I wrote my poem, but it seemed to come across a bit flat. I wrote a note at the top of the poem to the reader, saying that it should be read more quickly as it went along. In my mind, that captured the spirit of it. At the next English lesson the teacher stood in front of the class.

:ter has suggested I read his faster as I go along.'
,ne laughed when he made a rolling-of-the-eyes
ٮٮٮ ssion. I don't think he actually read it out.

That's a bit of a depressing thought to end on. If agents and publishers are no more than schoolteachers then I have no chance. However, in my experience, there is always someone who can look around the corner of the current market, and spot a new commercial opportunity coming up rapidly from behind. I hope so. If not, with the world of self-publishing and an inspired marketing campaign, anything could, and probably will, happen!

10th December 2016

Season's Greetings!

I thought I'd let the star of the novel provisionally titled *At Reception* offer you a seasonal greeting! Click/tap on it to expand the picture. It's also available as a high-resolution and PDF download below. I'm happy for you to print it off or share it. There's a lot of activity going on behind the scenes – a publishing update will be given shortly!

> *'Flowers, in the northern hemisphere it's snowing and the holiday season. Here summer is approaching and brings with it my birthday.'*
>
> *Celebrations are not a part of my life. Living alone, with no family and friends, I only share special times with my stuffed toy pets and those poor animals at the rescue centre. At work we*

occasionally exchange gifts for the holiday season, but it's not personal, it's work. As much as my colleagues feel like family when I am there, I know they are not. They are never at my home. As I am paid a minimum wage, my rent and bills use up all my money. The glamour of the hotel is not the reality of life for the workers. My simple existence is all I can afford. Not having to buy gifts is one less stress in my life. I am happy to keep it that way.

Note: I included this less-than-joyous text in my season's greetings cards. This was the first time people had the chance to hear from Sally. See the website for the actual picture.

1st January 2017

Happy New Year!

I thought I'd let the star of the novel provisionally titled *At Reception* offer you a New Year greeting! Click/tap on it to expand the picture. It's also available as a PDF download below. I'm happy for you to print it off or share it. There's a lot of activity going on behind the scenes – a publishing update will be given later this month!

Well, here we go again, another week at work, another week like all the rest in the year. Definitely a red-and-black checked ribbon day today! Nothing in my life has changed in the last week, month, even years. Every week like all the others. I don't mind that, I know where I stand. No doubt this week will bring a new set of events, characters, chat-up lines and challenges to exhaust me. Having to be nice to people all day, which I take seriously as it is my job, is mentally tiring. The constant barrage of having to say one thing but really thinking another is tough. You know me, when I get tired I am tempted to let rip, but I always seem to hold on and just make it to the end of the day without upsetting anyone!

I'll be OK, I will make it through.

Note: Following the success of the season's greetings card, I decided to repeat the concept with a New Year quote from Sally. See the website for the actual picture.

16th January 2017

Finding a New Best Friend

Monday

Someone invites you to a party. You hardly know the person, but hey, why not go? Maybe you'll meet a new best friend.

You arrive at the door feeling a little apprehensive. You don't know what's behind it. Will you enjoy yourself? *Stop it*, you say, *I'm an adult*. You touch the door and it swings open. You stand there frozen. You look for a familiar face, anyone you can latch onto. Nothing. You feel nervous, you feel the stares of people. Maybe I should leave now, but if I walk away they'll think I'm weird. Get a drink, just get a drink, walk around a bit and sneak out later.

So, how many new potential best friends would you make that night? One, maybe two you think worth seeing again? Maybe everyone! Or maybe none. Maybe you would not invest the time to get to know anyone. You would politely chat, and then leave as soon as you no longer feel the eyes watching you.

The next morning you tell people there were so many people there you had no chance to get to know anyone. How you didn't feel that oh-so-necessary connection to anyone, nor the event itself. It's going to be so hard to find a new best friend. I'll stick to the old ones.

Tuesday

Someone invites you to dinner at a new restaurant. You don't particularly know the person, but you would like to try the place so say yes. Maybe you will find a new favourite dish.

You arrive at the restaurant feeling uneasy. The decor is not familiar, it's supposed to be modern international, but to you it doesn't fit in any category. Not even fusion, which should cover everything. You push open the door and look around. You cannot see your host. You feel the stares of people looking at you, wondering why you are just standing there, frozen. You go to the bar to wait.

Your guest apologises for their late arrival, the traffic is so bad around here. *Bollocks*, you think, *everyone says that. You should have left earlier*. You both take your table.

You look at the menu. Your host suggests you select from the 'chef's specials'. Nothing grabs your attention. Nothing familiar you feel you can relate to. *Why did I bother making the effort?* you say to yourself. Eventually you select a couple of safe, standard dishes.

The next morning you tell people that the menu was too varied to decide what to eat. How you never found a new favourite dish. How you'll stick to the old ones.

Wednesday

Someone gives you a book. 'You'll love it,' they say. You've read the work of only a few authors, you like them. Why would you try something new? But hey, maybe you'll find a new favourite author.

You look at the cover. You already feel uneasy. It's not familiar. The name of the author, the design. No, this is not your kind of book. You read the back cover. *No, I don't like realism, I only like old-fashioned romance novels.*

You sigh. *Damn, I said I would read it, so I guess I have to open it.*

The dedication page says, *To Laena and all guest service agents, my thoughts are with you.*

You think, *Well, the author wrote it for somebody. Why would he write about a hotel receptionist? What's interesting about that?*

The next day you tell people how you now have a new best friend. Not the writer, no, but that poor girl. The one... *At Reception*!

Note: At this stage Sally's death was not included in the text. Whilst writing it was better to ignore her death, as it was the transformation of the person that was important, the reason for writing *At Reception*. Once I decided Sally had to die, I added her death as the last words I typed.